Stories *for* You

Selected and introduced by Barrie Wade

ARNOLD-WHEATON

Arnold-Wheaton
A Division of E J Arnold & Son Limited
Parkside Lane, Leeds LS11 5TD

A member of the Pergamon Group
Headington Hill Hall, Oxford OX3 0BW

First published by Arnold-Wheaton 1986

Printed in Great Britain by A. Wheaton & Co. Ltd, Hennock Road, Exeter

ISBN 0 560-09042-0

For Imogen and Miranda

Contents

Acknowledgements

The editor and publishers wish to thank the following who have kindly given permission for the use of copyright material:

J. M. Dent & Sons Ltd for Margaret Mahy's 'The Playground' from *The First Margaret Mahy Story Book*

Harper & Row, Publishers, Inc. for Natalie Savage Carlson's 'Jean Labadie's Big Black Dog' from *The Talking Cat and other stories of French Canada* copyright © 1952 by Natalie Savage Carlson

A. M. Heath & Company Ltd for Helen Cresswell's 'The Big Sunday Afternoon Bang' from *The Cat-Flap and the Apple Pie and other funny stories* published by W. H. Allen & Co. plc and for Michael Baldwin's 'The Snail Collector' from *Grandad with Snails* published by Routledge and Kegan Paul

Heinemann Educational Books for 'The Third Thing' from *The Talking Machine and other stories* by W. C. H. Chalk (Booster Book Series)

Lansdowne-Rigby, Publishers, for Colin Thiele's 'The Lock Out' from *The Rim of the Morning*

Longman Group Ltd for George Layton's 'The Balaclava Story' from *A Northern Childhood: The Balaclava Story and other stories* (Longman 'Knockouts' Series)

Penguin Books Ltd for Philippa Pearce's 'A Hamster at Large' from *The Elm Street Lot* (Kestrel Books 1979) pp 22-34, copyright © Philippa Pearce 1969, 1974, 1979; for Philippa Pearce's 'The Shadow-Cage' from *The Shadow-Cage and other tales of the Supernatural* (Kestrel Books 1977) pp 9-29, copyright © Philippa Pearce 1977; and for Bernard Ashley's 'Lenny's Red-Letter Day' from *I'm Trying to Tell You* (Kestrel Books 1981) pp 57-79, copyright © Bernard Ashley 1981

A. D. Peters & Co. Ltd for Bill Naughton's 'Spit Nolan' from *The Goalkeeper's Revenge* published by George Harrap & Sons Ltd

Laurence Pollinger Ltd and the William Saroyan Literary Foundation for William Saroyan's 'The Summer of the Beautiful White Horse' from *Best Stories of William Saroyan*

A. P. Watt Ltd and The Trustees of the Wodehouse Trust No. 3 and Century Hutchinson Ltd for P. G. Wodehouse's 'The Mixer'

Introduction

Stories are a powerful force in our lives. We tell them to other people about our experiences and we listen to those that people tell us. We use stories to make sense of the world and to give us pleasure and insight. A new story can take us into other people's lives and into experiences we have never had. It can let us see how like other people we are, or how different. Stories can be talked about, retold, changed or used for our own purposes. Through them we can look back into the past or forwards into the future. Above all they give us pleasure.

The stories here are selected primarily because of the pleasure they continue to give not only to me but to the children who have shared them with me. Of course pleasure is not the same as fun, although some of the stories do have funny parts. I can still hear the laughter in many a classroom as I re-read them for this collection. Other stories are touched with sadness, regret, unkindness, even cruelty. Some are exciting, gripping or scarey; others enchanting or comic. Often the feelings are mixed; for stories let us see that our world is not always simply drawn in black and white; it can also be a place full of complex emotions where we need to appreciate other people's feelings as well as our own.

Apart from the varieties of pleasure they afford, I have chosen these stories because they are worth reading more than once. They make good 'reading aloud' and I have found they make ideal material for reading together in classrooms. The shared experiences they provide are worth talking about. Discussion provides an important chance to match pupils' own experiences and feelings to those in the stories, thus increasing understanding.

I am grateful to many people for their help, encouragement and constructive comments. To my wife, Ann, to Hazel Hyde, Margaret Hier, Judith Elkin and all the pupils I have shared the stories with, I am indebted. One nine-year-old and one twelve-year-old in particular read all these stories and many more and gave me their frank comments. This book is dedicated to them.

Barrie Wade

A Hamster at Large

Philippa Pearce

In the beginning there were no hamsters in Elm Street at all. Plenty of other pets, of course: dogs, cats, budgerigars, tortoises, and so on. Every one of the Elm Street lot had a pet, even if it was only Jimmy Clegg's caterpillars.

Everyone except Ginger Jones. It wasn't that the Joneses couldn't afford to keep an animal or bird of some kind — especially as Ginger was the only child, and his father had a good job on the railways, and his mother had always been a manager. Perhaps a bit too managing, people said. Even the dustbin men were frightened of her. She had a way of putting things, rather stately, and often sharp.

Ginger longed for a pet, but his mother always said the same thing: "I have a husband and a son, both bringing dirt into the house and needing constant attention, day in, day out, week after week. I don't want another creature." So no dog or cat or anything else for Ginger Jones.

"What about a hamster?" Sim Tolland had once said to Ginger. For although nobody in Elm Street owned a hamster, everyone knew they weren't much trouble, because Woodside School always has a hamster.

Ginger shook his head hopelessly. "Day in, day out," he quoted, "week after week, month after month, year after . . ."

Then Sim Tolland had his brainwave. You see, the Woodside hamster can never stay in the school in holiday-time — there's no one regularly to look after her. (This

1

particular hamster was a female, called Elaine, after the school cook.) So, in holiday-time, one of the children — a different one each time — takes her home and looks after her until term starts again. Sim's brainwave was that Ginger Jones should take Elaine home. His mother couldn't object to a *temporary* hamster; and the idea was that Elaine would give Mrs Jones a taste, so to speak, of hamsters. A nice taste, of course. She'd see what pretty, clean creatures they are. How little they eat. How little room a hamster's cage takes up; and so on.

Careful preparations were needed at Woodside. To begin with, every one of the Elm Street lot swore an oath not to offer, against Ginger, to take Elaine. As for children from other streets — they had to be persuaded to keep their mouths shut and their hands down when the teacher asked for a volunteer. You could offer them marbles or chewing-gum or iced lollies or peanuts, or you could offer to make them into mincemeat.

This part of the plan went well. At the end of term Miss Borwich said: "Well, now, who wants Elaine this time?"

Absolute silence; absolute stillness. One or two of the children went pale with the strain; and somebody poked Ginger to wake him up. But he wasn't day-dreaming; just temporarily dazed. It had been arranged that he should speak up in a loud, clear, trustworthy voice; but all that came out was a creaky whisper: "Me. I'll take her."

"No one else offering?" Miss Borwich said in surprise. She looked round at everybody, and everybody stared back at her, willing her to hand Elaine over to Ginger. She looked at Ginger, and he managed a trustworthy smile.

"Well," Miss Borwich said uneasily, "Herbert Jones is the only one to volunteer — "

"He is," said Sim Tolland.

"Then he must take Elaine. I'm sure Herbert will take great

care of her." Ginger nodded as if his head were coming loose. "And you others," Miss Borwich said sternly, "I hope this doesn't mean you're losing your interest in Nature."

"Oh, no, Miss Borwich!" everyone said gratefully.

So Ginger took Elaine home.

Now Elaine really was a beauty — Ginger said she could have been a beauty queen. She was nearly as big as half a pound of butter, and in parts not far off the same colour. She had bright little black eyes — only Mrs Jones called them beady — and she had a nice character. Quite soon Ginger taught her to run up his arm on to his shoulder and then, standing on her hind legs, to reach for some favourite food — a sunflower seed or a cornflake — which he had lodged behind his ear. There was a little exercise-wheel in Elaine's cage, and every evening she would get on to it and pedal it round: *creak! creak! creak!* Mr Jones said the sound got on his nerves. He called the wheel her treadmill, although no one *made* Elaine go on it, of course. Mr Jones wasn't really a nervy man by nature; but he'd been a prisoner-of-war in the last war, and he said that when he saw Elaine standing on her hind feet up at the bars, it gave him a funny feeling.

Partly because of that, partly because he'd have done anything for Elaine, Ginger decided to make her a bigger, grander cage than the school one. He knew what he was doing, and the new cage, when it was finished, was fit for a princess, with all kinds of little improvements. One thing turned out to be not an improvement: Ginger backed the cage with wood, without any wire-mesh reinforcement. Soft wood, too; and in the night Elaine gnawed a hole right through it and escaped. Disappeared.

Ginger was very much upset, and so was his mother. Ginger thought that Elaine might starve; and Mrs Jones said, on the contrary, she couldn't bear the idea of that hamster running loose in the house and *fingering* everything

3

eatable. She also said she lay awake at night hearing Elaine climbing up the legs of the bed.

Ginger's father said nothing, but he wouldn't help to look for Elaine.

That Sunday morning, early, there was a commotion from the house next door to the Joneses', where the Cleggs live. The Cleggs' front door was flung open and Mrs Clegg rushed out into the street. She was holding an opened cornflake packet in her hand, and she seemed to be shaking the packet wildly, and screaming. It was just as if she were getting an electric shock from the packet, but couldn't break the contact and get rid of the thing. It turned out that the cornflake packet was being shaken *from the inside*; not by Mrs Clegg at all. When Mrs Clegg recovered enough presence of mind to throw the packet from her, skimming it along the street, out popped Elaine. Out she popped, and under Sim Tolland's big brother's second-hand car.

With Mrs Clegg having hysterics in the middle of Elm Street, everyone got to know what was going on. In a matter of seconds Ginger Jones and the rest of the Elm Street lot were on their hands and knees, peering under the car as best they could for the plastic sheeting that covered it.

"I can see her!" said Ginger.

"If you mean that yellowish thing," said Sim Tolland, "it looks more like an old banana-skin to me."

"I'd know her anywhere," said Ginger. "It's her."

"Whatever it is," said someone else, "it's not moving."

"She's petrified with fright," said Ginger. "We shall have to move the car to get her."

They had to move Mrs Clegg first, who was still laughing and sobbing about the packet of cornflakes. Then, having got the car key, they opened the door, took off the brake, and pushed the car out of its old position. All that time Ginger was on his stomach, watching the yellowish blur, saying, no,

4

she wasn't moving, and he only hoped she hadn't died of fright.

When they'd got the car away, they found that the yellowish blur was an old curled up banana-skin; and they noticed a kind of overhang to the kerb of the pavement there, and Elaine must have run along under that — right away, and heaven knew where she was now.

For several days there was no sign whatsoever of Elaine. (It turned out later that she must have wandered away into one of the other streets whose gardens or yards back on to Elm Street.) Ginger was very low-spirited indeed. He said that he knew in his bones that one of the Elm Street cats had mistaken Elaine for a mouse, and eaten her.

Then, after several days, people in Elm Street began to complain of odd noises that might be rats or mice, but weren't; hamster-hoards of food were found. Elaine was back.

Hamsters like travelling, especially by tunnel, and it can't have been too difficult in the terrace houses of Elm Street, especially with lofts whose partition walls are old and sometimes in bad condition. Elaine was seen only twice in the next few weeks. Once was by old Mr Crackenthorpe, when he was attending to the water-tank in his roof. He saw her and shouted at her: "You get out, or I'll boil you for my tea!" Elaine did get out.

And then Ginger saw her. He was at the elm stump by himself and very melancholy. Everyone else had gone off to the park, but he simply hadn't the heart for it. The sparrows were pecking about as usual, because the Elm Street lot often pass round, say biscuits or peanuts, and then there are crumbs. Today someone had spilt some popcorn.

It was very quiet, and Ginger was leaning sadly against the stump without moving. And then, with his downcast eyes, he saw Elaine — saw her come creeping out of the tree-stump itself, between his very feet. He held his breath and watched her; she collected several of the pieces of popcorn in her cheek-pouches and then slipped back by the way she had come.

He stooped to examine the bottom of the tree-stump. There was a hole that must be Elaine's front doorway. It was big enough for Ginger to get two fingers in — and then Elaine bit them. But they had been in long enough to touch more than Elaine: she had babies with her. That's why it's certain that she had spent some time out of Elm Street, where there were no other hamsters, and met a male hamster also on the run, and mated with him.

Now she had babies — there were nine of them. Ginger, with Sim Tolland, managed to get the whole family out of the stump and back into the old cage.

The cage was then kept in the Tollands' house. When the babies were old enough, Ginger and Sim gave them away, up and down Elm Street, and what with those hamsters and their descendants, there are always hamsters in Elm Street nowadays.

As for Elaine, Ginger took her back to Woodside at the end of the holidays. Miss Borwich, when she heard about the babies, said that she hoped the experience would be a warning to Elaine.

And Ginger? It would have been nice to have ended the story with Ginger's mother welcoming one of Elaine's babies into their home; but Mrs Jones said another hamster would enter the house only over her dead body.

So Ginger would have ended as he began, without a pet, if it hadn't been for the burglary. Burglars broke into the Joneses' house one Saturday afternoon when everyone was out. They didn't take anything much, but they made a mess of everything, and Mrs Jones was very, very much upset:

she washed everything in the house that was washable, and disinfected everything else. She put a notice on the gate saying, "Beware of the dog", and she hung a dog's lead and muzzle in the hall, where anyone could see who looked through the letter-box. She even kept a bowl of water in sight there, with DOG written round the bowl. Still she didn't feel safe, so, in the end, without telling Ginger — it was the biggest and best surprise of his life — she made Mr Jones buy a dog. Biter (that was what Mrs Jones said the dog must be called) was huge, with the wolfish look of an Alsatian and the bay of a bloodhound. His nature was timid but affectionate. He loved Ginger, and Ginger loved him: Biter was Ginger's dog.

The Balaclava Story

George Layton

Tony and Barry both had one. I reckon half the kids in our class had one. But I didn't. My mum wouldn't even listen to me.

"You're not having a balaclava! What do you want a balaclava for in the middle of summer?"

I must've told her about ten times why I wanted a balaclava.

"I want one so's I can join the Balaclava Boys . . ."

"Go and wash your hands for tea, and don't be so silly."

She turned away from me to lay the table, so I put the curse of the middle finger on her. This was pointing both your middle fingers at somebody when they weren't looking. Tony had started it when Miss Taylor gave him a hundred lines for flicking paper pellets at Jennifer Greenwood. He had to write out a hundred times: "I must not fire missiles because it is dangerous and liable to cause damage to someone's eye."

Tony tried to tell Miss Taylor that he hadn't fired a missile, he'd just flicked a paper pellet, but she threw a piece of chalk at him and told him to shut up.

"Don't just stand there — wash your hands."

"Eh?"

"Don't say 'eh', say 'pardon'. "

"What?"

"Just hurry up, and make sure the dirt comes off in the water, and not on the towel, do you hear?"

Ooh, my mum. She didn't half go on sometimes.

"I don't know what you get up to at school. How do you get so dirty?"

I knew exactly the kind of balaclava I wanted. One just like Tony's, a sort of yellowy-brown. His dad had given it to him because of his earache. Mind you, he didn't like wearing it at first. At school he'd given it to Barry to wear and got it back before home-time. But, all the other lads started asking if they could have a wear of it, so Tony took it back and said from then on nobody but him could wear it, not even Barry. Barry told him he wasn't bothered because he was going to get a balaclava of his own, and so did some of the other lads. And that's how it started — the Balaclava Boys.

It wasn't a gang really. I mean they didn't have meetings or anything life that. They just went around together wearing their balaclavas, and if you didn't have one you couldn't go around with them. Tony and Barry were my best friends, but because I didn't have a balaclava, they wouldn't let me go round with them. I tried.

"Aw, go on, Barry, let us walk round with you."

"No, you can't. You're not a Balaclava Boy."

"Aw, go on."

"No."

"Please."

I don't know why I wanted to walk round with them anyway. All they did was wander up and down the playground dressed in their rotten balaclavas. It was daft.

"Go on, Barry, be a sport."

"I've told you. You're not a Balaclava Boy. You've got to have a balaclava. If you get one, you can join."

"But I can't, Barry. My mum won't let me have one."

"Hard luck."

"You're rotten."

Then he went off with the others. I wasn't half fed up. All

my friends were in the Balaclava Boys. All the lads in my class except me. Wasn't fair. The bell went for the next lesson — ooh heck, handicraft with the Miseryguts Garnett — then it was home-time. All the Balaclava Boys were going in and I followed them.

"Hey, Tony, do you want to go down the woods after school?"

"No, I'm going round with the Balaclava Boys."

"Oh."

Blooming Balaclava Boys. Why wouldn't *my mum* buy *me* a *balaclava*? Didn't she realise that I was losing all my friends, and just because she wouldn't buy me one?

"Eh, Tony, we can go goose-gogging—you know, by those great gooseberry bushes at the other end of the woods."

"I've told you, I can't."

"Yes, I know, but I thought you might want to go goose-gogging."

"Well, I would, but I can't."

I wondered if Barry would be going as well.

"Is Barry going round with the Balaclava Boys an' all?"

"Course he is."

"Oh."

Blooming balaclavas. I wish they'd never been invented.

"Why won't your mum get you one?"

"I don't know. She says it's daft wearing a balaclava in the middle of summer. She won't let me have one."

"I found mine at home up in our attic."

Tony unwrapped some chewing-gum and asked me if I wanted a piece.

"No thanks." I'd've only had to wrap it in my handerkerchief once we got in the classroom. You couldn't get away with anything with Mr Garnett.

"Hey, maybe you could find one in your attic."

For a minute I wasn't sure what he was talking about.

"Find what?"

"A balaclava."

"No, we haven't even got an attic."

I didn't half find handicraft class boring. All that mucking about with compasses and rulers. Or else it was weaving, and you got all tangled up with balls of wool. I was just no good at handicraft and Mr Garnett agreed with me. Today was worse than ever. We were painting pictures and we had to call it "My favourite story". Tony was painting *Noddy in Toyland*. I told him he'd get into trouble.

"Garnett'll do you."

"Why? It's my favourite story."

"Yes, but I don't think he'll believe you."

Tony looked ever so hurt.

"But honest. It's my favourite story. Anyway what are you doing?"

He leaned over to have a look at my favourite story.

"Have you read it, Tony?"

"I don't know. What is it?"

"It's *Robinson Crusoe*, what do you think it is?"

He just looked at my painting.

"Oh, I see it now. Oh yes, I get it now. I couldn't make it out for a minute. Oh yes, there's Man Friday behind him."

"Get your finger off, it's still wet. And that isn't Man Friday, it's a coconut tree. And you've smudged it."

We were using some stuff called poster paint, and I got covered in it. I was getting it everywhere, so I asked Mr Garnett if I could go for a wash. He gets annoyed when you ask to be excused, but he could see I'd got it all over my hands, so he said I could go, but told me to be quick.

The washbasins were in the boys' cloakroom just outside the main hall. I got most of the paint off and as I was drying my hands, that's when it happened. I don't know what came over me. As soon as I saw that balaclava lying there on the floor, I decided to pinch it. I couldn't help it. I just knew that this was my only chance. I've never pinched anything before — I don't think I have — but I didn't think of this as . . . well . . . I don't even like saying it, but . . . well stealing. I just did it.

I picked it up, went to my coat, and put it in the pocket. At least I tried to put it in the pocket but it bulged out, so I pushed it down the inside of the sleeve. My head was throbbing, and even though I'd just dried my hands, they were all wet from sweating. If only I'd thought a bit first. But it all happened so quickly. I went back to the classroom, and as I was going in I began to realise what I'd done. I'd *stolen* a balaclava. I didn't even know whose it was, but as I stood in the doorway I couldn't believe I'd done it. If only I could go back. In fact I thought I would but then Mr Garnett told me to hurry up and sit down. As I was going back to my desk I felt as if all the lads knew what I'd done. How could they? Maybe somebody had seen me. No! Yes! How *could* they? They could. Of course they couldn't. No, course not. What if they did though? Oh heck.

I thought home-time would never come but when the bell did ring I got out as quick as I could. I was going to put the balaclava back before anybody noticed; but as I got to the cloakroom I heard Norbert Lightowler shout out that someone had pinched his balaclava. Nobody took much notice, thank goodness, and I heard Tony say to him that he'd most likely lost it. Norbert said he hadn't but he went off to make sure it wasn't in the classroom.

I tried to be all casual and took my coat, but I didn't dare put it on in case the balaclava popped out of the sleeve. I said tarah to Tony.

"Tarah, Tony, see you tomorrow."

"Yeh, tarah."

Oh, it was good to get out in the open air. I couldn't wait

to get home and get rid of that blooming balaclava. Why had I gone and done a stupid thing like that? Norbert Lightowler was sure to report it to the Headmaster, and there'd be an announcement about it at morning assembly and the culprit would be asked to own up. I was running home as fast as I could. I wanted to stop and take out the balaclava and chuck it away, but I didn't dare. The faster I ran, the faster my head was filled with thoughts. I could give it back to Norbert. You know, say I'd taken it by mistake. No, he'd never believe me. None of the lads would believe me. Everybody knew how much I wanted to be a Balaclava Boy. I'd have to get rid of the blooming thing as fast as I could.

My mum wasn't back from work when I got home, thank goodness, so as soon as I shut the front door, I put my hand down the sleeve of my coat for the balaclava. There was nothing there. That was funny, I was sure I'd put it down that sleeve. I tried down the other sleeve, and there was still nothing there. Maybe I'd got the wrong coat. No, it was my coat all right. Oh, blimey, I must've lost it while I was running home. I was glad in a way. I was going to have to get rid of it, now it was gone. I only hoped nobody had seen it drop out, but, oh, I was glad to be rid of it. Mind you, I was dreading going to school next morning. Norbert'll probably have reported it by now. Well, I wasn't going to own up. I didn't mind the cane, it wasn't that, but if you owned up, you had to go up on the stage in front of the whole school. Well I was going to forget about it now and nobody would ever know that I'd pinched that blooming lousy balaclava.

I started to do my homework, but I couldn't concentrate. I kept thinking about assembly next morning. What if I went all red and everybody else noticed? They'd know I'd pinched it then. I tried to think about other things, nice things. I thought about bed. I just wanted to go to sleep. To go to bed and sleep. Then I thought about my mum; what she'd say if she knew I'd been stealing. But I still couldn't forget about assembly next day. I went into the kitchen and peeled some potatoes for my mum. She was ever so pleased when she came in from work and said I must've known she'd brought me a present.

"Oh, thanks. What've you got me?"

She gave me a paper bag and when I opened it I couldn't believe my eyes — a blooming balaclava.

"There you are, now you won't be left out and you can stop making my life a misery."

"Thanks, Mum."

If only my mum knew she was making *my* life a misery. The balaclava she'd bought me was just like the one I'd pinched. I felt sick. I didn't want it. I couldn't wear it now. If I did, everybody would say it was Norbert Lightowler's. Even if they didn't, I just couldn't wear it. I wouldn't feel it was mine. I had to get rid of it. I went outside and put it down the lavatory. I had to pull the chain three times before it went away. It's a good job we've got an outside lavatory or else my mum would have wondered what was wrong with me.

I could hardly eat my tea.

"What's wrong with you? Aren't you hungry?"

"No, not much."

"What've you been eating? You've been eating sweets haven't you?"

"No, I don't feel hungry."

"Don't you feel well?"

"I'm all right."

I wasn't, I felt terrible. I told my mum I was going upstairs to work on my model aeroplane.

"Well, it's my bingo night, so make yourself some cocoa before you go to bed."

I went upstairs to bed, and after a while I fell asleep. The last thing I remember, was a big balaclava, with a smiling face, and it was the Headmaster's face.

I was scared stiff when I went to school next morning. In assembly it seemed different. All the boys were looking at me. Norbert Lightowler pushed past and didn't say anything. When prayers finished I just stood there waiting for the Headmaster to ask for the culprit to own up, but he was talking about the school fête. And then he said he had something very important to announce and I could feel myself going red. My ears were burning like anything and I was going hot and cold both at the same time.

"I'm very pleased to announce that the school football team has won the inter-league cup . . ."

And that was the end of assembly, except that we were told to go and play in the schoolyard until we were called in, because there was a teachers' meeting. I couldn't understand why I hadn't been found out yet, but I still didn't feel any better, I'd probably be called to the Headmaster's room later on.

I went out into the yard. Everybody was happy because we were having extra playtime. I could see all the Balaclava Boys going round together. Then I saw Norbert Lightowler was one of them. I couldn't be sure it was Norbert because he had a balaclava on, so I had to go up close to him. Yes, it was Norbert. He must have bought a new balaclava that morning.

"Have you bought a new one then, Norbert?"

"Y'what?"

"You've bought a new balaclava, have you?"

"What are you talking about?"

"Your balaclava. You've got a new balaclava haven't you?"

"No, I never lost it, at all. Some fool had shoved it down the sleeve of my raincoat."

The Big
Sunday Afternoon Bang

Helen Cresswell

What Sunday afternoons needed was a big bang, and this Sunday the children were determined that there should be one.

It was Peter's idea. He was the eldest, though not always the one who had the best ideas. Emma, who was two years younger, had good ideas, too. (It had been her idea to turn the yard into a roller skating rink, for instance, and charge the other kids to come in.) But Peter had a more scientific brain than either Emma or Daisy (who, being only five, could hardly be expected to have a scientific brain, yet).

"This afternoon," he told Emma on the way back from Sunday School, "we're really going to shake things up."

"Are we?" Emma was interested, all right, but still not properly into the Sunday afternoon feeling of desperation and boredom. She was wearing her best green embroidered smock and was watching her black patent shoes flash in and out under its hem. She was also still being Sunday School teacher's pet — which she certainly was. This was not her fault. She happened to like stories, and Bible ones were as good as any others.

"It could be dangerous," Peter said. "It's an experiment."

"All right," she agreed absently. "We'll do it."

By the time dinner was over she was ready, as usual, for anything. Sunday afternoons, the children agreed, were truly awful. It was almost as if something actually happened to make time stop — if anything, it seemed to go backwards.

On Sunday afternoon their parents went to sleep. They did not call it sleeping. They called it 'having five minutes' — which anyone could see was wrong. Their mother actually went up and lay on the bed. Their father, after a look at the paper, sank back in the armchair and shut his eyes. Usually he snored.

This particular Sunday was in June, and it was sunny. This meant that they were allowed in the garden as long as they did not play games, and kept their voices down to whispers. (This was because the Westbys, who lived next door, had 'five minutes', too.)

"What we're going to do," Peter told them, in the corner of the rockery, behind the laurel, "is make an explosion!"

The other two stared. Daisy did not even know what an explosion was. Emma did, and felt bound to be cautious.

"How do we know it won't blow *us* up?" she asked. This seemed the most important question to ask.

"We don't," he replied. "It's an experiment to make the most almighty bang that'll wake everybody up for miles around. We're going to mix up things that I don't suppose anyone's ever mixed up before, and we don't know *what'll* happen. All I'm saying is, I *hope* it'll go off with a bang!"

"I want to mix," said Daisy instantly. Mixing was one of her favourite things to do.

"What kind of things are we going to mix?" Emma asked.

"Anything we can lay our hands on. We'll wait till they're both asleep, and then go back in. If we stand on a kitchen chair, we can get to all those packets and bottles in the cupboard. There's lots of stuff up there — real stuff, from the chemist's."

"Where will we mix it? What if we blow the house up?"

"I've thought of that," he said. "We'll dig a hole, here in the garden, and sink a basin into it, and then mix in that."

"What *sort* of things, though?" she persisted.

"Oh — mustard, salt, vinegar, washing up liquid, milk, floor polish — anything we can find. There's bound to be some chemicals in some of them, and it'll just be a matter of hitting the right mixture."

Emma thought. A girl at school had told her only last week that it was dangerous to eat oranges and milk together. She said it curdled in the stomach and made poison. This had sounded very likely to Emma, and so she had stopped taking oranges to school.

"Well — I'm going to!" Peter got up. "Please yourself!"

There was no choice, really. She was, of course, as much in favour of a big bang as he was. She was just not keen on being blown up herself. But by now the special Sunday quiet had already descended like a blight over the whole neighbourhood. Even the birds were subdued, as if they had been warned of the consequences of loud whistling on a Sunday afternoon.

"Come on, then." She followed him.

"Let's mix!" agreed Daisy happily, and tailed after them.

They tiptoed into the house. It was depressingly quiet. They could only hear the buzzing of a fly and the sound of their father's snoring from the next room.

"Right!"

Carefully Peter edged a chair across the lino and, standing on it, began to hand down bottles, packets and tins. He fetched down nearly everything off the third shelf. Emma stared at it all, awestruck.

"Boracic," she read on one packet. "Bicarbonate of soda. *Should* we, do you think?"

"Not in *here*, idiot! I told you — in the garden. Now go and get some of those little plastic building cup things of Daisy's. We'll tip a bit of everything into each, then take it all out on a tray."

Once the actual work began, Emma enjoyed it. She

measured liquids and powders into the multi-coloured cups. She used a mustard spoon, because it seemed safer. She noticed that Peter was using a soup spoon, shovelling out the ingredients with an abandon that was a little alarming. To keep Daisy quiet, they gave her a bottle of washing up liquid and let her squirt it into a jam jar. She enjoyed this very much and it could not possibly, Emma thought, be dangerous. The first trayful ready, they took it out to the garden.

"Now — where shall we have the hole?"

"Not too near the house," said Emma instantly.

"Not *too* near," he agreed. "Here, look, by the hedge."

He took the trowel and began to dig out a hole between the hedge and the hollyhocks.

"We'd better have it pretty deep," he said. "You keep watch and make sure no one's looking."

Emma stared about her. The gardens were quiet. She looked up at her mother's curtained window, then at the Westbys'. There was no sign of life anywhere. The whole world, it seemed, was having 'five minutes'. Daisy was making a hole of her own, using a spoon.

"Right!" said Peter at last. Carefully he fitted a plastic mixing bowl into the hole. He picked up two of the little cups, hesitated, then threw the contents in. Emma gasped. He carried on, tipping things in and then stirring with a long stick. He paused.

"Nothing's happened." Emma did not know whether to be pleased or sorry.

"Not likely to," he said. "That was only the dry stuff. It's when we start putting the liquids in that things'll start to happen."

He took a yellowish liquid — cough mixture? — leaned well back from the hole, and threw it in. They waited, then bent over and looked.

"It certainly looks horrible," said Emma. "Ugh — and can you smell it?"

A thought struck her.

"Could it turn into poison gas, do you think?"

"Could," he said. "Better keep back as much as we can. Lucky we're outside. People only really get overcome by fumes inside."

All the time Peter was stirring in the liquids, Emma's heart was thudding. She thought how brave he was, crouching there over that foreign, unpredictable mixture. Then everything had gone. They waited.

"I don't think there's going to be an explosion," said Emma at last.

They sat there. Had it not been a Sunday afternoon, they might even have left it at that. But it was, and teatime was still light years away. The gardens lay deserted under the hot sun.

"Come on!" Peter sprang up. "There's lots more stuff left to try. We'll hit the right mixture, sooner or later!"

After that a kind of madness took hold of them. They went into the pantry and took some of nearly everything, from currants to tomato sauce. Emma even broke an egg into the hole. It floated on the evil brown mixture like a wicked yellow eye. After that she became giggly, because it seemed to her that what they were making now was a kind of omelette — and omelettes do not blow up.

Peter simply became silent. He was absolutely absorbed, intent on explosion. He still believed that it would come, in the end. "It won't *half* be a bang," he muttered, now and again. *"Won't* there be a bang!"

On one of his trips back from the house he actually brought a whole tin of something with him.

"Stand back," he ordered. *"This'll* do it!"

Emma did not obey him as she would have done earlier.

She merely watched with interest as he spooned a great heap of white powder into the brownish liquid in the bowl.

"Ooooooeeeeh!"

Emma's scream was so loud and long that she actually heard it herself, and clapped her hands over her ears to shut it out. She ran then, towards the house, still screaming and still seeing that awful foaming, seething mass.

"What — what the — ?" Her father was there, redfaced and dazed and already furious. Peter came up beside her, the tin still in his hands.

"Idiot!" he hissed. "It was only fizzy liver salts!"

"Look!" It was Daisy speaking, from the pantry. They looked. Emma screamed again. Daisy was covered in blood.

It was not blood at all, as it turned out. It was tomato sauce. It was all over the pantry floor as well, and so were a whole bag of flour, a couple of packets of tea and a lot of sugar and gravy salt. Here and there floated the evil yellow eyes of eggs.

"I mixed," said Daisy happily.

Then their parents were both there, both bad-tempered from so rude an interruption of their 'five minutes' — both, in fact, livid.

Emma and Peter exchanged glances. There *was* going to be an explosion that Sunday, after all . . .

The Third Thing

W.C.H. Chalk

JOHN DIGBY was a small boy. He was not only small, he was also thin and rather weak. He was twelve years old, he wore glasses and his clothes were patched. His face was pale and his nose was long, his hair was untidy and he had pimples on his face.

He had no friends for he did not like games very much; he was never put into a team of any sort; he had no hobbies which were interesting to other boys; he did not go camping, or fishing, or bird-watching. He did not have a bicycle, nor did he have a record-player. He never had anything to swop, he never had any tricks to play, he never got into trouble at school, or out of it.

"He's a drip," said Mick Moakes, of Form 3c. Mick Moakes had no time for 'drips' and the 'drips' at Queens Road School knew it. They kept well away from Mick Moakes and his pals.

Moakes was the biggest bully in the school and he had a little gang of boys around him who took orders from him and gave presents to him now and again. If they didn't, Moakes would set the other members of his gang on to them. This Moakes fellow was almost fifteen; a big, hulking, loutish boy always ready with his fists and boots to make smaller boys jump to his orders. Even the prefects were afraid of him.

For a long time he had taken no notice of John Digby. The lad seemed harmless and nobody ever bothered with him; he just came and went as he pleased, not getting in anybody's way.

One day John Digby was sitting in the playground eating his lunch from a paper bag when a dark shadow loomed over him. He looked up and saw Mick Moakes peering down at him. Behind Moakes stood Sam Green and Joe Brady, two of his pals. They were grinning and John knew that something was going to happen. To him . . .

" 'Allo, Four-eyes," said Moakes, sitting down beside John. "What you got there, something nice to eat?"

Sam Green and Joe Brady began to close in. John began to feel scared. Moakes peered into the paper bag.

"Look at all this grub," he said, helping himself to a sandwich. "D'you want a sandwich, Sam? Would you like one, Joe?" He handed each of his pals a sandwich and the three of them munched away until they had eaten them.

"Anything else? No cakes? I like cakes. So does Sam and Joe. You'll have to bring some cakes tomorrow, Digby." Moakes pushed his face close to John's and grinned. The smaller boy shrank back in fear. He looked round, hoping that a teacher may have seen what had happened but Sam Green and Joe Brady blocked out his view. Moakes came closer.

"Oh, yes . . . ! We don't like little drips who go around telling tales to teachers, do we? D'you know what happens to little drips who do that? We bash 'em!"

"That's right," grinned Sam Green. "We meet 'em outside and take 'em over the Park."

They left him then and went to look for someone else who had some sandwiches left. John was terrified.

For the rest of that day he sat in his desk wondering what he should do. He wanted to tell someone about it but then he remembered what Moakes and his pals had said about bashing him.

That evening, he told his father about it. His father listened for a little while, then said, "Look, John . . . you'll have to stand on your own feet and fight your own battles. It's no good running to me with every little tale. You lash out at them; a bully always runs away when somebody stands up to him."

So next day John Digby waited in the playground with his bag of sandwiches. It was not long before Moakes and his pals came across. Sam Green and Joe Brady stood in front of him while Mick Moakes grabbed the bag.

"My dad says . . ." began John. Moakes looked up, his mouth filled with bread. Somehow, seeing Moakes with his mouth stuffed with his sandwich made John see red. He drew back his small fist and punched Moakes on the nose as hard as he could!

Moakes took the punch and fell back on the bench. Blood poured from his nose and he let out a yell which made John's blood run cold.

Sam jumped on him and pinned his arms to his sides. Joe Brady started hitting him with his fists. Moakes mopped up the blood from his nose with a handkerchief. A crowd of boys began to gather round and Mr Wilson could be seen coming across towards them.

Someone spotted him and gave the alarm. Moakes and his pals fled away but not before Joe Brady had told John what to expect if he told Mr Wilson what had happened. The small boy's body hurt where Joe's fists had struck him but he told Mr Wilson that he had only been larking about.

When school was over at four o'clock, John looked carefully up and down the road outside the main gate before leaving. There was no sign of Moakes and his pals so he walked off down the road towards his home.

Just a little way along the road there was an alley which led to the Park. Moakes stepped out from the alley just as John passed and grabbed him. Sam Green and Joe Brady took an arm each and rushed him into the Park.

They took him into a clump of bushes and left him alone with Moakes while they kept watch.

John didn't stand a chance. The fifteen year old lad flew at him with fists and feet flying. When he was down in the dirt, Moakes kicked him in the ribs. He pulled him up to his feet and stood him against a tree. He drew his big fist back and John fainted with fright. Moakes let him slump in the dust and walked away with his pals, chuckling and sniggering.

From that day onwards, John Digby's life at school was a misery. Not a day passed without Moakes coming over and sneering at him. Sam Green tripped him up whenever he could, Joe Brady took his glasses and bent the frame into a twisted shape, Moakes jeered at him and called him "Four-eyes". Soon, it became his nickname and every boy in the school called him by it.

Moakes and his pals took a delight in telling the school about his fainting. ". . . I just waved my fist at him and he fainted away." Soon, some of the other lads began to act the story whenever John was around; they would pretend to faint and fall down when their friends wagged a finger at them. John began to hate the school and longed for the day to come when he could leave it for good.

He was really afraid of Moakes and his bullies. Whenever he saw them coming, he would look round for a place to hide from them and they would drag him out to torment him again. It did not take Moakes long to realise that he could have a lot of fun this way. It was better than hitting the smaller boy; you only had to pretend to hit him and he'd start crying and snivelling. Then you could make him beg for mercy. Crowds of boys would gather to watch John Digby drop on to his knees before Mick Moakes.

"Beg for mercy, Four-eyes . . ." he would yell, and in the end he always did, with his hands held together and tears streaming from his eyes.

Poor John! Every day had its terrors for him. He never knew what new stunt Moakes & Co. had planned for him. They took his money from him, ate his lunch, stole his books, broke his pens, ripped his jacket. And always they jeered at him.

They found out that his birthday was on the seventh of July and they made up a party to bump him, after school. All that day, they left him alone. No tricks were played on him; no one pulled his hair or called out after him. He was allowed to eat his lunch in peace and by the time school was over for the day he had begun to think that his days of terror were over.

He walked along the road that afternoon and, without thinking, passed the alley which led to the Park.

Suddenly, they jumped out on him and hustled him into the Park between them. There Moakes was waiting.

"Happy birthday to you . . ." sang Moakes, grabbing his arms.

"Happy birthday to you . . ." sang Sam Green, taking his legs.

"Happy birthday, dear Four-eyes . . ." sang Joe Brady with the others as they flung him into the air. They caught him as he came down and flung him up again, singing all the while.

"Now we'll bump you," cried Moakes. "Thirteen times . . ." Again and again they thumped his thin body on to the hard ground. His glasses fell off and Joe stepped on them.

"Oops, sorry! I've broken them," he sneered. Mick Moakes went to a bush and came back with a bunch of stinging nettles.

"Here's our present to you, Four-eyes," he said and pushed the bunch down the back of John's neck while Sam held the shirt collar open.

They took his new fountain pen from him, shook him until the nettles were well down inside his shirt, then slapped his back while they wished him many happy returns of the day.

John collapsed on the ground, wriggling and twisting in pain. His cries were so loud that a man began to walk over to the bushes and Moakes & Co., having had their fun, ran off.

The man who found John behind the bushes stood for a moment, looking down at the sobbing boy. Between the deep sobs, he was able to make out what had been done to him and he pulled several handfuls of thick, soft dock-leaves while John took his shirt off. The man crushed the dock-leaves and rubbed them gently into the boy's back. Slowly, the burning pain began to die away.

John dried his eyes and put his shirt on again watched all the while by the kindly stranger.

The man had white hair and very blue eyes. He seemed to be listening to every word that John said but spoke very little himself. Bit by bit, he got the whole story out of the boy and still said nothing when John had finished. They walked off along the road together and it was not until they had reached the road where John lived that the stranger spoke.

"I am going to help you," he said. "Many years ago, when I was in China, I met an old Chinaman who became my closest friend. He let me into a secret and made me promise never to reveal this secret to anyone . . . except if it was a case of helping a person to defend himself against a tyrant. Do you know what a tyrant is, John Digby?"

"Someone like Moakes, you mean?"

"Yes. Moakes and his bullies are tyrants. The old Chinaman gave me the secret of power. It is a very, very dangerous secret."

"Why?"

The stranger felt in his pocket and took out a little green bottle. It had a silver stopper.

"Power is a very dangerous thing," he said. "It may be good to have power over men; it may be evil if that power is used wrongly. In this bottle there is a secret drug. Whoever drinks this drug becomes enormously strong for about five minutes, stronger than any other man on Earth!"

John stopped, his eyes wide open and shining. "You mean . . . I could lick Moakes and his pals in a fight?"

The stranger nodded slowly. "Yes, easily. But remember, the power will last only for a little while. After that, it will go for good. This is the last bottle of the drug and once it has been used, there will be no more."

He pressed the bottle into the boy's hand with a final word of warning. "Don't take the drug until thirty seconds before you need it."

John Digby went to sleep that night with the little green bottle under his pillow. He forgot his stinging back and the bruises on his body. He went to sleep muttering Moakes's name and woke up the next morning with the name ringing inside his head.

The little green bottle was in his pocket when he went to school and he had a grim smile on his face as he sat in the classroom.

Moakes and his little gang were waiting for him in the

playground when dinner time came. There was a crowd of boys hanging about, waiting for the fun to begin.

Joe Brady came over. "Got a new pair of glasses, I see. Did you have them for your birthday?"

Sam Green peered over Joe's shoulder. "Did you have a nice birthday party, Four-eyes? Did you get bumped?"

Now Moakes came up to join his pals. The crowd of boys drew nearer, trying to catch every word. John looked round at their faces. His hands were trembling as he opened his bag of sandwiches.

Mick Moakes took one. "I hear you had a birthday treat yesterday afternoon," he said, loudly. "Someone gave you a nice present, didn't they? What was it, Four-eyes? Tell us."

The crowd of boys pressed closer. Moakes grinned round at them, pleased to find that so many were listening to him. He went on: "You mustn't eat all those sandwiches. It might bring you out in a nettle-rash!"

Joe Brady burst out laughing at this. "Yes . . . have you ever had nettle-rash, Four-eyes?"

Sam Green looked at Mick Moakes, grinning. "I reckon he must have had it, sometime. If you ask me, he's still got it. His face is all pimply."

Moakes nodded. "That's right, Sam. Now, I know how to get rid of nettle-rash. Funny thing, you can get rid of it by rubbing the skin with fresh nettles — like these!"

And from behind his back he brought out a branch of green nettles. He was wearing gloves, John noticed.

John Digby shrank away from him. Moakes came closer and the playground seemed to be filled with boys, all trying to see what would happen.

They saw the small boy huddled up in a corner of the bench, his bag of sandwiches scattered on the ground. Moakes was bending over him, holding the nettles near his face. Sam and Joe were watching, ready to leap in and help their leader. John Digby took out a little green bottle and pulled out the silver stopper. He tipped the bottle into his mouth.

"What's that stuff?" growled Moakes. "Cod liver oil?"

"Yellow liver oil," said Sam Green. He was always funny.

The crowd of boys came closer, wondering what would happen now. Someone said that Four-eyes had poisoned himself and the word 'poison' went from mouth to mouth. Mr Wilson heard it as he began to push his way into the crowd.

He got to the middle of the crowd just in time to see John Digby leap to his feet, his eyes blazing. The small boy whipped off his jacket and gave it to another boy to hold.

"Here, what's going on?" snapped Mr Wilson, and then stopped. For John Digby sprang at Mick Moakes like a tiger. He swept away the nettles with one sweep of his arm and crashed his fist into the bully's face. Moakes staggered back, roaring. Sam Green jumped at the small boy and met a fist which shot out like a piston rod and hit him on the jaw with a sharp crack which could be heard all over the playground. Without stopping, John Digby went for Joe Brady and smacked a punch under his ear which made Joe's teeth rattle. Joe sagged at the knees and began to sink slowly downwards.

Moakes came back at John Digby, fists flying like a windmill. John ducked, rose again swiftly and somehow Mick's jaw collided with the small boy's head. Also, the small boy's fists were thudding into Moakes's ribs with a rapid drumming sound. Mr Wilson's eyes goggled at the speed and force which those blows carried. Moakes made funny noises and he reeled back under the rain of punches until he fell on to the bench.

John Digby wheeled round to meet Sam Green and clouted him on the side of his head with a blow which sent him staggering. The small boy spun around to face Joe who was slowly coming up from his knees. He should have stayed there, for next moment he was sent over on his back by a tremendous uppercut from John Digby's fist. It came up like a hammer and the thud of it made Mr Wilson gasp with amazement.

How was it possible, he wondered, for an undersized little shrimp like this to pack such a wallop in those skinny fists. He watched the little fellow as he tore into the bully, Moakes, without seeming to draw a fresh breath.

Moakes went down under a hail of punches which battered into his face. He put up his hands to defend himself and was pushed back off the bench. John followed, hurling himself at Moakes like a wild cat, and slamming blow after blow into the bully's swollen face. Behind him, Sam Green stood up and rushed to his leader's aid. Mr Wilson darted forward to stop him.

He saw Sam's foot come back, ready to kick. He slipped his hand under the lifted leg and jerked it upwards. Sam gave a yell and fell on his face. Mr Wilson dragged him to his feet and Sam became still.

Joe Brady was picking up some of his teeth from the playground when the prefects grabbed him. From behind the bench John Digby stood up, peering at the crowd and asking for his glasses. The crowd of boys fell back open-mouthed as Mr Wilson lifted Mick Moakes on to the bench.

Both his eyes were closing fast as big blue bruises swelled up over them. His jaw sagged open and blood ran from the corner of a cut lip. His face was a mass of bruises and he was wheezing like an old horse.

John Digby walked away, wiping his glasses on his tie

and panting deeply. Mr Wilson ran after him and grabbed him just as he collapsed into his arms . . .

Later on, when some of the fuss had died down Mr Wilson made John tell him the whole story. He listened to the bit about the secret drug and shook his head slowly.

"That can't be true, John," he said. "There's no such drug."

"Well, you saw for yourself that it worked, sir!"

"True, but it sounds a tall story to me."

"It's not, sir! I met the strange man again, after the fight. I told him that the drug worked and I asked him what it was made from."

John Digby frowned. "Well . . . it's rather funny, really. He said that the drug was made from three things. The first thing was water."

"Water? What was the second thing?"

"Sugar. Yes, sir! Sugar, that's all. That was the second thing."

"And what was the third thing? Did he tell you?"

The boy nodded, still frowning. "Yes, sir! The man looked at me and said that the Third Thing was Faith! What did he mean by that, sir?"

Mr Wilson didn't answer.

The Lock Out

Colin Thiele

By eleven o'clock that night Jim realised how slowly time went when you were on your own. Boomer called in for a while before tea to make sure Jim would be fit for the big match in the morning, but apart from that he spent the evening alone. He washed the dishes, fed the cat, watched TV, polished his boots, put out the milk bottles, locked the door and sauntered about restlessly from room to room. It was a shock to see how dark and empty the house could be. Then, at the last minute, he remembered that his football shorts hadn't been washed after Thursday's practice, so he hastily doused them in detergent and warm water, rubbed the slide marks and dirty patches from the seat and then drew them out looking over-scrubbed and bleached. After rinsing them and squeezing them as dry as he could, he carried them up to the lounge, turned on the gas fire and hung the shorts over a chair to dry. He would have to iron them in the morning before the match. Ginger, the big tortoise-shell cat, flopped down in front of the fire with her engine going and her tail swishing in gentle ecstasy. For a while they enjoyed each other's company with silent relish, watching the steam rising from the drying shorts.

The warm moisture gave Jim an idea — a hot bath. He looked at his watch. It was late, almost midnight, but he would sleep all the better for it. And so, by the time he had filled the bath, wallowed in it like a grampus, soaped himself three times, tested the way his legs suddenly grew heavier when he lifted them out of the water, measured the length of the hair on his shins, trimmed his toenails with his mother's nail scissors and finally dried himself vigorously, it was past midnight.

But if he thought that Friday the thirteenth had finished with him now, he was very much mistaken. The worst disaster of all was about to happen. He was standing on the bathmat, trying to dry the small of his back by rubbing it against the towel like an itchy horse against a tree, when he heard Ginger coughing. She had run out of the lounge and now stood urgently at the front door, waiting to be let out, retching and coughing like a consumptive chain-smoker.

"Oh, my gosh!" Jim thought. "Fur-balling or biliousness." He suddenly remembered his mother's ominous warning: "If the cat wants to go outside, for heaven's sake don't keep it waiting." He leapt to the front door, swung it back and held open the wrought-iron screen. But with a strangely feminine perversity the cat only ran forward a pace or two before crouching and convulsing again.

"Not there! Shoo! Ahh, for Pete's sake!" Jim hastily tied the towel round his waist, flicked off the light switch to avoid being exposed to public view and swept her up in his hands.

"Out you go, whether you like it or not!" He ran across the veranda in his bare feet and tossed her gently on to the garden.

"Off you go! Shoo!"

As he turned to slip back inside again the breeze stirred; the hibiscus swayed by the steps, and the shadows moved in the street lights. Then gently, very gently, the front door swung shut and the latch sprang into the lock with a soft click. Horrified, Jim ran to the door, pushing and heaving. But he was too late. He was locked out. Locked out of his own house, at midnight, and without any clothes on.

For a second or two he cowered, appalled, in the corner of the veranda. But what had seemed so dim and secluded at first soon became more and more exposed as his eyes grew accustomed to the dark. Luckily there was nobody about. The street was deserted, the neighbours were all in bed. Although Jim's mind was still strangely numb, one thought charged about in it like a bull in a yard. He had to get back inside – this instant, before anyone saw him.

His only hope was an unlatched window. He skirted the hibiscus bush in the corner of the garden and made for the dining room. It looked out over the front lawn and held a long view up the curve of the street, but at least there was an off chance that the window there might be unlocked. As he stepped onto the soft grass of the lawn he was astonished to find himself walking on tip-toe. For a second he was vaguely aware of his own tension, a kind of catching himself by surprise before he plunged off across the grass.

For the first three strides the spring of the lawn under his feet was urgently pleasant, but at the fourth step he trod sharply on the garden hose not a foot from the end near the sprinkler, and a squirt of icy water shot out like an electric shock. He leapt up with a noisy gasp and ran to the window. But it was locked. He groaned at the thoroughness of his mother's anti-burglar precautions and stood indecisively for a second, cold drops and runnels of water pausing and chasing down his calves.

Suddenly a car swung into the street and came bearing down on the house, its headlamps boring at him like a searchlight. Too late Jim realised that he was being floodlit like a marble statue in the park, and he flung himself down, commando-style, on the lawn. The car took the curve at speed, and its slashing blade of light swung over him like a scimitar. Jim rose uncertainly to his feet, the soft prickle of the lawn stippling his chest and belly. It was a curiously cold, grassy feeling, but it seemed to salve the hot flush of his embarrassment and shame.

He ran for the other windows along the front of the house, testing each one in turn. They were all locked. Twice more a car raked the house with its headlights, and twice more Jim had to take violent evasive action. The second time, in flinging himself down recklessly behind the espaliered roses, he landed on some old cuttings that his mother had left lying there after her pruning. He only just resisted the impulse to yell and leap up, rolling over on his side in silent agony instead, his fingers trying to seal the cat's-claw scratches down his ribs. The girl in the car turned to her companion enquiringly:

"Darling, what was that thing in the garden there?"

"Dunno. Dog, I s'pose."

"But it looked sort of long and white. Like a pig."

"Ah-h, use your sense, Rosie. How could a white pig be running round the suburbs at this time of night?"

By the time Jim had probed the front and side of the house he was sore and exhausted. But fear drove him on. His only hope now lay in the windows at the back – in the kitchen, laundry and toilet. But these looked down the steeply sloping back garden where the ground fell away. They were over half a metre beyond his reach. He looked round for a box or stool, but of course his mother was much too careful to have left anything like that lying about the place. Despair began to numb his mind again, just as the creeping goose-pimples on his skin seemed

36

to tighten and contract his body. And then, in a sort of despairing mental lunge, he thought of Mr Hogan's stepladder.

Ben Hogan next door was a good-natured little man who often lent things to the Bears. Jim himself had sometimes borrowed the stepladder from the old shed behind the tank. But there was the problem of getting it out and carrying it back. He couldn't possibly go round by the front gate, without clothes, at this time of night. It would have to be over the back fence – wooden palings two metres high, unpainted and needled all over with long splinters. But a desperate plight called for desperate action.

Happily the two timber cross-pieces that held up the palings were on Jim's side, and he was able to get a foothold on them and swing a leg over the top. Then, with a sudden heave, he hoisted himself up, skinning his calves and thighs, until he was balanced unstably on top. He tied the towel more firmly round his waist and leapt – a kind of dismounting, bucking movement that deposited him on Mrs Hogan's beans with a thud. He quickly disentangled himself and crept over to the woodshed.

For a while it looked as if his luck had changed. The ladder was there right enough, and he managed to half drag, half carry it across to the fence. This time it was going to be a lot easier; he could use the ladder to help himself over.

He stood the steps against the palings and climbed to the top; but here he struck unforeseen trouble, for how was he going to balance himself up there while he transferred the ladder from one side of the fence to the other? He tried squatting down on the paling-tops with one leg on each side, using the cross-bar as a brace for his left foot, but he couldn't get enough leverage that way, and in any case if his foot slipped he had a fair chance of bisecting himself.

He pondered the Archimedean problem, crouched there, riding the fence like a jockey. There was only one thing for it: he would have to stand up to get the extra purchase, and pull the ladder over in seesaw fashion. He jiggled himself along for a metre or so until he reached one of the square wooden posts that held up the fence. There he managed to get himself shakily erect while he slowly turned round for the ladder. But the constant twisting and shuffling was too much for the towel round his middle. As he stood up and heaved, the single knot slipped open suddenly and the towel fell swiftly and silently down into Hogan's garden. And at that moment Mrs Hogan, no less fearful of burglars than Jim's mother, and convinced that she could hear stealthy noises in the back garden, pushed open the screen-door and pointed a rather etiolated beam of torchlight at Jim.

"W. . . who's there?" she demanded, with a queer, quavering truculence. Jim froze. Caught by surprise he could think of nothing more effective to do than to become a statue. A riot of vague pictures from his history lessons tumbled about in his mind − the Elgin marbles, the Laocoön, Hercules. . . He stood stock still, bent forward, naked and precarious on top of the fence, goose-pimples of cold and terror popping out on his buttocks.

Mrs Hogan's yellow torch-beam fell short of him, but a diffused glow caught the fence and endowed Jim with a ghostly lack of substance − a kind of moonlit statuary in suburbia. Mrs Hogan suddenly spotted its vague whiteness and, with a sound that was both gurgle and gasp, retreated in terror. She stumbled to the phone and, after trying to dial with three fingers at once, finally got through to the police.

Meanwhile a scarred and panting Jim, having finished using the paling fence as a pedestal, hastily dragged the ladder into his yard and pushed it against the kitchen window. But when he climbed up to open it at last, the window wouldn't budge. Refusing to believe that it, too, had been locked by his all-suspecting mother, he rattled it furiously. But it held firm. He thumped again with his fists – and then realised with sudden fear that he was making more noise than Macduff knocking at the gates in Inverness. He shrank away from the window and crept down the ladder again. A spasm of shivering swept over him, and his teeth chattered.

Then he saw something. Standing upright in his father's potato patch was a four-pronged garden fork – the perfect lever to wedge in under the stubborn window. He ran over, dragged it from the ground and climbed back up the ladder. It was fairly easy to push the points of the prongs into the narrow slit between the frame and the window, but in his eagerness he didn't wedge them in far enough, so that when he bore down heavily on the handle, the tines suddenly splintered out of the wood and he all but dived headlong on to the gravel below. He saved himself by a frenzied and lucky clutch at the sill while the fork gonged like a bass tuning-fork against the concrete foundations beneath.

Jim hung there breathless for a second, but a spark of hope still glimmered with the moonshine on the tines. He descended, picked up the fork and returned to the attack. This time he would make sure that he had the maximum possible purchase without the wood giving way. Twice he drove the tines in with what strength he could, but each time as he pressed down tentatively on the handle he felt them slipping out again. It would need a sudden vicious jab. He swung back and thrust the fork in sharply like a bayonet. But there were four points instead of one, and somehow the fork seemed to turn in his hand as he thrust. There was a grating crack, a clash of falling fragments as one of the tines struck glass instead of wood, and the window gaped emptily in front of him. Jim stared at it unbelievingly. Then he laughed – a sobbing laugh of incredulity and relief. For there was the opening! All he had to do was to crawl through it to safety and peace. In the morning he could get a pane of glass, fit it with tacks and putty and there it was. Who would ever know?

A car raced up the street and stopped. Doors opened and footsteps hurried about the paths. Some went into Hogan's next door, and there was the sound of low and urgent consultation. Jim, still clutching the fork, crouched in the shadow on top of his ladder. The voices stopped and more footsteps crunched on the gravel. Some came over towards the fence and Jim froze against the wall in terror. Then, quite suddenly, a strong beam of light flashed onto him, and two policemen stood in the drive below.

"There he is!"

"Look out!"

"Move in slowly!"

"Watch that fork!"

Jim made a strangled sound as the policemen slowly moved in, never dousing the merciless glare of their torches for an instant. It didn't occur to him that a naked young man brandishing a digging fork on top of a ladder at midnight would scarcely look either modest or peace-loving. He felt ruthlessly exposed, a violent sense of intrusion, and tried unsuccessfully to hide behind the handle of the fork. At the same time he knew it was essential to say something reassuring, to explain the whole business simply and clearly. But the best he could manage was "I . . . I . . ." Two more policemen joined in the blockade and all four closed in steadily. They didn't say a word. Jim's mouth went on working until suddenly he surprised himself by announcing in a high squeak: "Look here, I'm Bear! Jim Bear!" The policemen either silently agreed or took it as a threat. For with a sudden rush they swept him from the ladder, flung off the fork and bundled him unceremoniously on his back in the strawberry patch.

"Grab him!"

But at that moment Jim came violently to life. He leapt to his feet and sped round the house like a gazelle. The heavy sergeant pounded after him, and two of the younger policemen ran up the drive to try to head him off. But Jim had a clear lead. He shot across the lawn, took the front fence at a stride, and raced out on to the street almost under the wheels of a car. He and the car swerved simultaneously. There was a shriek of a woman and a screeching of tyres.

"It's *him*!" the woman screamed. "It's the burglar!" There was a second of confusion as the police were cut off by the swerving driver. It was enough to give him the advantage. He swung back on to the footpath, hurdled Schuberts' fence next door, shot across their lawn, hurtled through two back gardens, then doubled back and crouched behind the creeper that sprawled along his own back fence. Luckily at the same moment a dog barked further up the street. It unwittingly acted as a decoy, and the footsteps and voices of his pursuers faded away hurriedly towards it.

Jim stood up cautiously and listened. No sound. He peered over the fence into the back garden. No sign. The stepladder still stood by the gaping kitchen window and the fork shone dimly in the garden strip below. Up to this point in his flight he had acted wholly by reflex and instinct; from the moment the policemen had appeared below him he hadn't planned so much as a gesture. But now his mind began working again, craftily. Doubling back on his tracks to outwit his pursuers had been good strategy. He had often seen it done on TV, so why not in real life?

Stealthily he hauled himself over the back fence and dropped down into his own back garden. There he paused, breathing cautiously. No sound or movement. With sudden resolution he tiptoed across the back lawn, leapt the strawberry patch, ran lightly up the stepladder and eased himself in through the broken window. The whole thing only took a couple of seconds. From the sill he lowered himself noiselessly inside, stepped gingerly for a metre or two, trying to avoid treading on broken glass, and then hurried down the darkness of the passage. His pyjamas were hanging on the bathroom rail. He put them on with a kind of breathless haste, the touch of clothing against his flesh suddenly filling him with a strange sense of security and gratitude. Then he padded quickly up to his room, got into bed and pulled the bedclothes high up round his shoulders.

Spit Nolan

Bill Naughton

Spit Nolan was a pal of mine. He was a thin lad with a bony face that was always pale, except for two rosy spots on his cheekbones. He had quick brown eyes, short, wiry hair, rather stooped shoulders, and we all knew that he had only one lung. He wasn't sorry for himself in any way, and in fact we envied him, because he never had to go to school.

Spit was the champion trolley-rider of Cotton Pocket; that was the district in which we lived. He had a very good balance, and sharp wits, and he was very brave, so that these qualities, when added to his skill as a rider, meant that no other boy could ever beat Spit on a trolley — and every lad had one.

Our trolleys were simple vehicles for getting a good ride downhill at a fast speed. To make one you had to get a stout piece of wood about five feet in length and eighteen inches wide. Then you needed four wheels, preferably two pairs, large ones for the back and smaller ones for the front. However, since we bought our wheels from the scrapyard, most trolleys had four odd wheels. Now you had to get a poker and put it in the fire until it was red hot, and then burn a hole through the wood at the front. Usually it would take three or four attempts to get the hole bored through. Through this hole you fitted the giant nut-and-bolt, which acted as a swivel for the steering. Fastened to the nut was a strip of wood, on to which the front axle was secured by bent nails. A piece of rope tied to each end of the axle served for steering. Next you had to paint a name on it: *Invincible* or *Dreadnought*, though it might be a motto: *Death before Dishonour* or *Labour and Wait*. That done, you then stuck your chest out, opened the back gate, and wheeled your trolley out to face the critical eyes of the world.

Spit spent most mornings trying out new speed gadgets on his trolley, or searching Enty's scrapyard for good wheels. Afternoons he would go off and have a spin down Cemetery Brew. This was a very steep road that led to the cemetery, and it was very popular with trolley-drivers as it was the only macadamised hill for miles around. Spit used to lie in wait for a coal-cart or other horse-drawn vehicle, then he would hitch *Egdam* to the back to take it up the brew. *Egdam* was a name in memory of a girl called Madge, whom he had once met at Southport Sanatorium, where he had spent three happy weeks. Only I knew the meaning of it, for he had reversed the letters of her name to keep his love a secret.

It happened that we were gathered at the street corner with our trolleys one summer evening when Ernie Haddock let out a hiccup of wonder: "Hy, chaps, wot's Leslie got?"

We all turned our eyes on Leslie Duckett, the plump son of the local publican. He approached us on a brand-new trolley, propelled by flicks of his foot on the pavement. Such a magnificent trolley had never been seen! The riding board was of solid oak, almost two inches thick; four new wheels with pneumatic tyres; a brake, a bell, a lamp, and a spotless steering-cord. In front was a plate on which was the name in bold lettering: *The British Queen*.

"It's called after the pub," remarked Leslie. He tried to edge it away from Spit's trolley, for it made *Egdam* appear horribly insignificant. Voices had been stilled for a minute, but now they broke out:

"Where'd it come from?"

"How much was it?"

"Who made it?"

Leslie tried to look modest. "My dad had it specially made to measure," he said, "by the gaffer of the Holt Engineering Works."

He was a nice lad, and now he wasn't sure whether to feel proud or ashamed. The fact was, nobody had ever had a trolley made by somebody else. Trolleys were swopped and so on, but no lad had ever owned one that had been made by other hands. We went quiet now, for Spit had calmly turned his attention to it, and was examining *The British Queen* with his expert eye. First he tilted it, so that one of the rear wheels was off the ground, and after giving it a flick of the finger he listened intently with his ear close to the hub.

"A beautiful ball-bearing race," he remarked, "it runs like silk." Next he turned his attenion to the body. "Grand piece of timber, Leslie — though a trifle on the heavy side. It'll take plenty of pulling up a brew."

"I can pull it," said Leslie, stiffening.

"You might find it a shade *front-heavy*," went on Spit.

"It's well made," said Leslie. "Eh Spit?"

Spit nodded. "Aye, all the bolts are countersunk," he said, "everything chamfered and fluted off to perfection. But — "

"But what?" asked Leslie.

"Do you want me to tell you?" asked Spit.

"Yes, I do," answered Leslie.

"Well, it's got none of *you* in it," said Spit.

"How do you mean?" says Leslie.

"Well, you haven't so much as given it a single tap with a hammer," said Spit. "That trolley will be a stranger to you to your dying day."

"How come," said Leslie, "since I *own* it?"

Spit shook his head. "You don't own it," he said, in a quiet, solemn tone. "You own nothing in this world except those things you have taken a hand in the making of, or else you've earned the money to buy them."

Leslie sat down on *The British Queen* to think this one out. We all sat round, scratching our heads.

"You've forgotten to mention one thing," said Ernie Haddock to Spit, "what about the *speed*?"

"Going down a steep hill," said Spit, "she should hold the road well — an' with wheels like that she should certainly be able to shift some."

"Think she could beat *Egdam*?" ventured Ernie.

"That," said Spit, "remains to be seen."

Ernie gave a shout: "A challenge race! *The British Queen* versus *Egdam*!"

Next Sunday, chattering like monkeys, eating bread, carrots, fruit and bits of toffee, the entire gang of us made our way along the silent Sunday-morning streets for the big race at Cemetery Brew. We were split into two fairly equal sides.

Leslie, in his serge Sunday suit, walked ahead, with Ernie Haddock pulling *The British Queen*, and a bunch of supporters around. They were optimistic, for Leslie had easily outpaced every other trolley during the week, though as yet he had not run against Spit.

Spit was in the middle of the group behind, and I was pulling *Egdam* and keeping the pace easy, for I wanted Spit to keep fresh. He walked in and out among us with an air of imperturbability that, considering the occasion, seemed almost godlike. It inspired a fanatical confidence in us. It was such that Chick Dale, a curly-headed kid with soft skin like a girl's, and a nervous lisp, climbed up on to the spiked railings of the cemetery, and, reaching out with his thin fingers, snatched a yellow rose. He ran in front of Spit and thrust it into a small hole in his jersey.

"I pwesent you with the wose of the winner!" he exclaimed.

"And I've a good mind to present you with a clout on the lug," replied Spit, "for pinching a flower from a cemetery. An' what's more, it's bad luck." Seeing Chick's face, he relented. "On second thoughts, Chick, I'll wear it. Ee, wot a 'eavenly smell!"

A faint sweated glow had come over Spit's face when we reached the top of the hill, but he was as majestically calm as ever. Taking the bottle of cold water from his trolley seat, he put it to his lips and rinsed out his mouth in the manner of a boxer.

The two contestants were called together by Ernie.

"No bumpin' or borin'," he said.

They nodded.

"The winner," he said, "is the first who puts the nose of his trolley past the cemetery gates."

They nodded.

"Now, who," he asked, "is to be judge?"

Leslie looked at me. "I've no objection to Bill," he said. "I know he's straight."

I hadn't realised I was, I thought, but by heck I will be!

"Ernie here," said Spit, "can be starter."

With that Leslie and Spit shook hands.

"Fly down to them gates," said Ernie to me. He had his father's pigeon-timing watch in his hand. "I'll be setting 'em off dead on the stroke of ten o'clock."

I hurried down to the gates. I looked back and saw the

supporters lining themselves on either side of the road. Leslie was sitting upright on *The British Queen*. Spit was settling himself to ride belly-down. Ernie Haddock, handkerchief raised in the right hand, eye gazing down on the watch in the left, was counting them off — just like when he tossed one of his father's pigeons.

"Five — four — three — two — one — off!"

Spit was away like a shot. That vigorous toe-push sent him clean ahead of Leslie. A volley of shouts went up from his supporters, and groans from Leslie's. I saw Spit move straight to the middle of the road camber. Then I ran ahead to take up my position at the winning-post.

When I turned again I was surprised to see that Spit had not increased the lead. In fact, it seemed that Leslie had begun to gain on him. Not that it seemed possible he could ever catch him. For Spit, lying flat on his trolley, moving with a fine balance, gliding, as it were, over the rough patches, looked to me as though he were a bird that might suddenly open out its wings and fly clean into the air.

The runners along the side could no longer keep up with the trolleys. And now, as they skimmed past the halfway mark, and came to the very steepest part, there was no doubt that Leslie was gaining. Spit had never ridden better; he coaxed *Egdam* over the tricky parts, swayed with her, gave her her head, and guided her. Yet Leslie, clinging grimly to the steering-rope of *The British Queen*, and riding the rougher part of the road, was actually drawing level. Those beautiful ball-bearing wheels, engineer-made, encased in oil, were holding the road, and bringing Leslie along faster than spirit and skill could carry Spit.

Dead level they sped into the final stretch. Spit's slight figure was poised fearlessly on his trolley, drawing the extremes of speed from her. Thundering beside him, anxious but determined, came Leslie. He was actually drawing ahead — and forcing his way to the top of the camber. On they came like two charioteers — Spit delicately edging to the side, to gain inches by the extra downward momentum. I kept my eyes fastened clean across the road as they came belting past the winning-post.

First past the plate was *The British Queen*. I saw that first. Then I saw the heavy rear wheel jog over a pothole and strike Spit's front wheel — sending him in a swerve across the road. Suddenly, then, from nowhere, a charabanc came speeding round the wide bend.

Spit was straight in its path. Nothing could avoid the collision. I gave a cry of fear as I saw the heavy solid tyre of the front wheel hit the trolley. Spit was flung up and his back hit the radiator. Then the driver stopped dead.

I got there first. Spit was lying on the macadam road on his side. His face was white and dusty, and coming out between his lips and trickling down his chin was a rivulet of fresh red blood. Scattered all about him were yellow rose petals.

"Not my fault," I heard the driver shouting. "I didn't have a chance. He came straight at me."

The next thing we were surrounded by women who had got out of the charabanc. And then Leslie and all the lads came up.

"Somebody send for an ambulance!" called a woman.

"I'll run an' tell the gatekeeper to telephone," said Ernie Haddock.

"I hadn't a chance," the driver explained to the women.

"A piece of his jersey on the starting handle there..." said someone.

"Don't move him," said the driver to a stout woman who had bent over Spit. "Wait for the ambulance."

"Hush up," she said. She knelt and put a silk scarf under Spit's head. Then she wiped his mouth with her little handkerchief.

He opened his eyes. Glazed they were, as though he couldn't see. A short cough came out of him, then he looked at me and his lips moved.

"Who won?"

"Thee!" blurted out Leslie. "Tha just licked me. Eh, Bill?"

"Aye," I said, "old *Egdam* just pipped *The British Queen.*"

Spit's eyes closed again. The women looked at each other. They nearly all had tears in their eyes. Then Spit looked up again, and his wise, knowing look came over his face. After a minute he spoke in a sharp whisper:

"Liars. I can remember seeing Leslie's back wheel hit my front 'un. I didn't win — I lost." He stared upward for a few seconds, then his eyes twitched and shut.

The driver kept repeating how it wasn't his fault, and next thing the ambulance came. Nearly all the women were crying now, and I saw the look that went between the two men who put Spit on a stretcher — but I couldn't believe he was dead. I had to go into the ambulance with the attendant to give him particulars. I went up the step and sat down inside and looked out the little window as the driver slammed the doors. I saw the driver holding Leslie as a witness. Chick Dale was lifting the smashed-up *Egdam* on to the body of *The British Queen.* People with bunches of flowers in their hands stared after us as we drove off. Then I heard the ambulance man asking me Spit's name. Then he touched me on the elbow with his pencil and said:

"Where *did* he live?"

I knew then. That word 'did' struck right into me. But for a minute I couldn't answer. I had to think hard, for the way he said it made it suddenly seem as though Spit Nolan had been dead and gone for ages.

The Playground

Margaret Mahy

Just where the river curled out to meet the sea was the town playground, and next to the playground in a tall cream-coloured house lived Linnet. Every day after school she stood for a while at her window watching the children over the fence, and longing to run out and join them. She could hear the squeak squeak of the swings going up and down, up and down all afternoon. She could see children bending their knees pushing themselves up into the sky. She would think to herself, "Yes, I'll go down now. I won't stop to think about it. I'll run out and have a turn on the slide," but then she would feel her hands getting hot and her stomach shivery, and she knew she was frightened again.

Jim her brother and Alison her sister (who was a year younger than Linnet) were not frightened of the playground. Alison could fly down the slide with her arms held wide, chuckling as she went. Jim would spin on the roundabout until he felt more like a top than a boy, then he would jump off and roll over in the grass shouting with laughter. But when Linnet went on the slide the smooth shiny wood burned the backs of her legs, and she shot off the end so fast she tumbled over and made all the other children laugh. When she went on the roundabout the trees and the sky smudged into one another and she felt sick. Even the swings frightened her and she held their chains so tightly that the links left red marks in her hands.

"Why should I be so scared?" she wondered. "If only I could get onto the swing and swing without thinking about it I'd be all right. Only babies fall off. I wouldn't mind being frightened of lions or wolves but it is terrible to be frightened of swings and seesaws."

Then a strange thing happened. Linnet's mother forgot to pull the blind down one night. The window was open and a little wind came in smelling of the ropes and tar on the wharf and of the salt sea beyond. Linnet sighed in her sleep and turned over. Then the moon began to set lower in the sky. It found her window and looked in at her. Linnet woke up.

The moonlight made everything quite different and enchanted. The river was pale and smooth and its other bank, the sandspit around which it twisted to find the sea, was absolutely black. The playground which was so noisy and crowded by day was deserted. It looked strange because it was so still and because the red roundabout, the green slide, and the blue swings were all grey in the moonlight. It looked like the ghost of a playground, or a faded clockwork toy waiting for daylight, and happy children to wind it up and set it going again. Linnet heard the town clock strike faintly. Midnight. She thought some of the moon silver must have got into the clock's works because it sounded softer, yet clearer than it did during the day. As she thought this she was startled to see shadows flicker over the face of the moon. "Witches?" she wondered before she had time to tell herself that witches were only make-believe people. Of course it wasn't witches. It was a flock of birds flying inland from the sea.

"They're going to land on the river bank," she thought. "How funny, I didn't know birds could fly at night. I suppose it is because it is such bright moonlight."

They landed and were lost to sight in a moment, but

53

just as she began to look somewhere else a new movement caught her eye and she looked back again. Out from under the trees fringing the river bank, from the very place where the birds had landed, came children running, bouncing and tumbling: their voices and laughter came to her, faint as chiming clock bells.

Linnet could see their bare feet shaking and crushing the grass, their wild floating hair, and even their mischievous shining eyes. They swarmed all over the playground. The swings began to swing, the seesaws started their up and down, the roundabout began to spin. The children laughed and played and frolicked while Linnet watched them, longing more than ever before to run out and join in the fun. It wasn't that she was afraid of the playground this time—it was just that she was shy. So she had to be content to stare while all the time the swings swept back and forth loaded with the midnight children, and still more children crowded the roundabout, the seesaw and the bars.

How long she watched Linnet could not say. She fell asleep watching, and woke up with her cheek on the window-sill. The morning playground was quite empty and was bright in its daytime colours once more.

"Was it all dreams?" wondered Linnet blinking over breakfast. "Will they come again tonight?"

"Wake up, stupid," Alison called. "It's time to be off. We'll be late for school."

All day Linnet wondered about the playground and the children playing there by moonlight. She seemed slower and quieter than ever. Jim and Alison teased her calling her Old Dreamy, but Linnet did not tell them what dreams she had.

That night the moon woke Linnet once more and she

sat up in a flash, peering out anxiously to see if the midnight children were there. The playground, colourless and strange in its nightdress, was empty, but within a minute Linnet heard the beat of wings in the night. Yes, there were the birds coming in from the sea, landing under the trees and, almost at once, there were the children, moonlit and laughing, running to the playground for their night games. Linnet leaned farther out of her window to watch them, and one of them suddenly saw her and pointed at her. All the children came and stood staring over the fence at her. For a few seconds they just stayed like that, Linnet peering out at them and the midnight children, moon-silver and smiling, looking back at her. Their hair, blown behind them by the wind, was as pale as sea foam. Their eyes were as dark and deep as sea caves and shone like stars.

Then the children began to beckon and wave and jump up and down with their arms half out to her, they began to skip and dance with delight. Linnet slid out of bed, climbed out of the window and over the fence all in her nightgown. The midnight children crowded up to her, caught her and whirled her away.

Linnet thought it was like dancing some strange dance. At one moment she was on the roundabout going round and round and giggling with the other children at the prickly dizzy feeling it gave her, in the next she was sweeping in a follow-my-leader down the slide. Then someone took her hand and she was on the seesaw with a child before her and a child behind and three more on the other end.

Up went the seesaw.

"Oh, I'm flying!" cried Linnet. Down went the seesaw. Bump went Linnet, and she laughed at the unexpected bouncy jolt when the seesaw end hit the rubber tyre beneath it. Then she was on the swing. She had never been so high before. It seemed to Linnet that at any moment the swing was going to break free and fly off on its own, maybe to the land where the midnight children came from. The swing felt like a great black horse plunging through the night, like a tall ship tossing over the green waves.

"Oh," cried Linnet, "it's like having wings." The children laughed with her, waved and smiled, and they swept around in their playground dance, but they didn't speak. Sometimes she heard them singing, but they were always too far away for her to hear the words.

When, suddenly, the midnight children left their games and started to run for the shadow of the trees, Linnet knew that for tonight at least she must go home as well, but she was too excited to feel sad. As she climbed through the window again she heard the beat of wings in the air and saw the birds flying back to the sea. She waved to them, but in the next moment they were quite gone, and she and the playground were alone again.

Next day when Alison and Jim set out for the playground Linnet said she was coming too. "Don't come to me if you fall off anything," said Jim scornfully.

Alison was kinder. "I'll help you on the roundabout," she said. "You hang on to me if you feel giddy."

"But I won't feel giddy!" Linnet said, and Alison stared at her, surprised to hear her so confident and happy. However, this was just the beginning of the surprises for Alison and Jim. Linnet went on the roundabout and sat there without hanging on at all. On the swing she went almost as high as the boys, and she sat on the seesaw with her arms folded.

"Gosh, Linnet's getting brave as anything over at the playground," said Jim at tea that night.

"I always knew she had it in her," said Daddy.

The next night, and the next, Linnet climbed out of her window and joined the beckoning children in the silver playground. During the day, these midnight hours seemed like enchanted dreams and not very real. All the same Linnet was happy and excited knowing she had a special secret all to herself. Her eyes sparkled, she laughed a lot, and got braver and braver in the playground until all the children stopped what they were doing to watch her.

"Gee, Mum," Alison said, "you should see Linnet. She goes higher on the swing than any of the boys—much higher than Jim. Right up almost over the top."

"I hope you're careful, dear," her mother said.

"I'm all right," Linnet cried. "I'm not the least bit scared."

"Linnet used to be frightened as anything," Alison said, "but now she's braver than anybody else."

Linnet's heart swelled with pride. She could hardly wait until the moon and the tide brought her wonderful laughing night-time companions. She wanted them to admire her and gasp at her as the other children did. They came as they had on other nights, and she scrambled over the fence to join them.

"Look at me!" she shouted, standing on the end of the seesaw and going up and down. The child on the other end laughed and stood up too, but on its hands, not on its feet. It stayed there not over-balancing at all. Linnet slid away as soon as she could and ran over to the swings. She worked herself up higher and higher until she thought she was lost among the stars far far above the playground and the world, all on her own.

"Look at me," she called again. "Look at me."

But the child on the next swing smiled over its shoulder

and went higher—just a little higher. Then Linnet lost her temper.

"It's cleverer for me," she shouted, "because I'm a real live child, but you—you're only a flock of birds."

Suddenly silence fell, the laughter died away, the singers stopped their songs. The swings swung lower, the roundabout turned slower, the seesaws stopped for a moment. Linnet saw all the children's pale faces turn towards her: then, without a sound, they began to run back to the shadow of the trees. Linnet felt cold with sadness. "Don't go," she called. "Please don't go." They did not seem to hear her.

"I'm sorry I said it," she cried after them, her voice sounding very small and thin in the moonlit silent playground. "I didn't mean it." But no—they would not stop even though she pleaded, "Don't go!" yet again. The playground was empty already and she knew she couldn't follow her midnight children. For the last time she spoke to them.

"I'm sorry!" she whispered and, although it was only a whisper, they must have heard because they answered her. Their voices and laughter drifted back happy and friendly saying their own goodbye. The next moment she saw for the last time the birds flying back over the sea to the secret land they came from. Linnet stood alone and barefooted in the playground, the wind pulling at her nightgown. How still and empty it was now. She pushed at a swing and it moved giving a sad little squeak that echoed all round. There was nothing for Linnet to do but go back to bed.

She was never afraid of the playground again and had lots and lots of happy days there laughing and chattering with her friends. Yet sometimes at night, when the moon rose and looked in at her window, she would wake up and look out at the playground just in case she should see the moon and the tide bringing her a flock of strange night-flying birds, which would turn into children and call her out to play with them. But the playground was always empty, the shining midnight children, with their songs and laughter, were gone forever.

Jean Labadie's Big Black Dog

Natalie Savage Carlson

Once in another time, Jean Labadie was the most popular storyteller in the parish. He acted out every story so that it would seem more real.

When he told about the great falls of Niagara, he made a booming noise deep in his throat and whirled his fists around each other. Then each listener could plainly hear the falls and see the white water churning and splashing as if it were about to pour down on his own head. But Jean Labadie had to stop telling his stories about the *loup-garou*, the demon who takes the shape of a terrible animal and pounces upon those foolish people who go out alone at night. Every time the storyteller dropped down on all fours, rolled his eyes, snorted, and clawed at the floor, his listeners ran away from him in terror.

It was only on the long winter evenings that Jean had time to tell these tales. All the rest of the year, he worked hard with his cows and his pigs and his chickens.

One day Jean Labadie noticed that his flock of chickens was getting smaller and smaller. He began to suspect that his neighbour, André Drouillard, was stealing them. Yet he never could catch André in the act.

For three nights running, Jean took his gun down from the wall and slept in the henhouse with his chickens. But the only thing that happened was that his hens were disturbed by having their feeder roost with them, and they stopped laying well. So Jean sighed and put his gun back and climbed into his own bed again.

One afternoon when Jean went to help his neighbour mow the weeds around his barn, he found a bunch of grey chicken feathers near the fence. Now he was sure that André was taking his chickens, for all of his neighbour's chickens were scrawny white things.

He did not know how to broach the matter to André without making an enemy of him. And when one lives in the country and needs help with many tasks, it is a great mistake to make an enemy of a close neighbour. Jean studied the matter as his scythe went swish, swish through the tall weeds. At last he thought of a way out.

"Have you seen my big black dog, André?" he asked his neighbour.

"What big black dog?" asked André. "I didn't know you had a dog."

"I just got him from the Indians," said Jean. "Someone has been stealing my chickens so I got myself a dog to protect them. He is a very fierce dog, bigger than a wolf and twice as wild."

Jean took one hand off the scythe and pointed to the ridge behind the barn.

"There he goes now," he cried, "with his big red tongue hanging out of his mouth. See him!"

André looked but could see nothing.

"Surely you must see him. He runs along so fast. He lifts one paw this way and another paw that way."

As Jean said this, he dropped the scythe and lifted first one hand in its black glove and then the other.

André looked at the black gloves going up and down like the paws of a big black dog. Then he looked toward the ridge. He grew excited.

"Yes, yes," he cried, "I do see him now. He is running

along the fence. He lifts one paw this way and another paw that way, just like you say."

Jean was pleased that he was such a good actor he could make André see a dog that didn't exist at all.

"Now that you have seen him," he said, "you will know him if you should meet. Give him a wide path and don't do anything that will make him suspicious. He is a very fierce watchdog."

André promised to stay a safe distance from the big black dog.

Jean Labadie was proud of himself over the success of his trick. No more chickens disappeared. It seemed that his problem was solved.

Then one day André greeted him with, "I saw your big black dog in the road today. He was running along lifting one paw this way and another paw that way. I got out of his way, you can bet my life!"

Jean Labadie was pleased and annoyed at the same time. Pleased that André believed so completely in the big black dog that he could actually see him. He was also annoyed because the big black dog had been running down the road when he should have been on the farm.

Another day André leaned over the fence.

"Good day, Jean Labadie," he said. "I saw your big black dog on the other side of the village. He was jumping over fences and bushes. Isn't it a bad thing for him to wander so far away? Someone might take him for the *loup-garou*."

Jean Labadie was disgusted with his neighbour's good imagination.

"André," he asked, "how can my dog be on the other side of the village when he is right here at home? See him walking through the yard, lifting one paw this way and another paw that way?"

André looked in Jean's yard with surprise.

"And so he is," he agreed. "My faith, what a one he is! He must run like lightning to get home so fast. Perhaps you should chain him up. Someone will surely mistake such a fast dog for the *loup-garou*."

Jean shrugged hopelessly.

"All right," he said, "perhaps you are right. I will chain him near the henhouse."

"They will be very happy to hear that in the village," said André. "Everyone is afraid of him. I have told them all about him, how big and fierce he is, how his long red tongue hangs out of his mouth and how he lifts one paw this way and another paw that way."

Jean was angry.

"I would thank you to leave my dog alone, André Drouillard," he said stiffly.

"Oh, ho, and that I do," retorted André. "But today on the road he growled and snapped at me. I would not be here to tell the story if I hadn't taken to a tall maple tree."

Jean Labadie pressed his lips together.

"Then I will chain him up this very moment." He gave a long low whistle. "Come, fellow! Here, fellow!"

André took to his heels.

Of course, this should have ended the matter, and Jean Labadie thought that it had. But one day when he went to the village to buy some nails for his roof, he ran into Madame Villeneuve in a great what-a-to-do of excitement.

"Jean Labadie," she cried to him, "you should be ashamed of yourself, letting that fierce dog run loose in the village."

"But my dog is chained up in the yard at home," said Jean.

"So André Drouillard told me," said Madame, "but he has broken loose. He is running along lifting one paw this way and another paw that way, with the broken chain dragging in the dust. He growled at me and bared his fangs. It's a lucky thing his chain caught on a bush or I would not be talking to you now."

Jean sighed.

"Perhaps I should get rid of my big black dog," he said. "Tomorrow I will take him back to the Indians."

So next day Jean hitched his horse to the cart and waited until he saw André Drouillard at work in his garden. Then he whistled loudly toward the yard, made a great show of helping his dog climb up between the wheels and drove past André's house with one arm curved out in a bow, as if it were around the dog's neck.

"*Au revoir*, André!" he called. Then he looked at the empty half of the seat. "Bark goodbye to André Drouillard, fellow, for you are leaving here forever."

Jean drove out to the Indian village and spent the day with his friends, eating and talking. It seemed a bad waste of time when there was so much to be done on the farm, but on the other hand, it was worth idling all day in order to end the big black dog matter.

Dusk was falling as he rounded the curve near his home. He saw the shadowy figure of André Drouillard waiting for him near his gate. A feeling of foreboding came over Jean.

"What is it?" he asked his neighbour. "Do you have some bad news for me?"

"It's about your big black dog," said André. "He has come back home. Indeed he beat you by an hour. It was that long ago I saw him running down the road to your house with his big red tongue hanging out of his mouth and lifting one paw this way and another paw that way."

Jean was filled with rage. For a twist of tobacco, he would have struck André with his horsewhip.

"André Drouillard," he shouted, "you are a liar! I just left the big black dog with the Indians. They have tied him up."

André sneered.

"A liar am I? We shall see who is the liar. Wait until the others see your big black dog running around again."

So Jean might as well have accused André of being a chicken thief in the first place, for now they were enemies anyway. And he certainly might as well have stayed home and fixed his roof.

Things turned out as his neighbour had hinted. Madame Villeneuve saw the big black dog running behind her house. Henri Dupuis saw him running around the corner of the store. Delphine Langlois even saw him running through the graveyard among the tombstones. And always as he ran along, he lifted one paw this way and another paw that way.

There came that day when Jean Labadie left his neighbour chopping wood all by himself, because they were no longer friends, and drove into the village to have his black mare shod. While he was sitting in front of the blacksmith shop, André Drouillard came galloping up at a great speed. He could scarcely hold the reins, for one hand was cut and bleeding.

A crowd quickly gathered.

"What is wrong, André Drouillard?" they asked.

"Have you cut yourself?"

"Where is Dr Brisson? Someone fetch Dr Brisson."

André Drouillard pointed his bleeding hand at Jean Labadie.

"His big black dog bit me," he accused. "Without warning, he jumped the fence as soon as Jean drove away and sank his teeth into my hand."

There was a gasp of horror from every throat. Jean

Labadie reddened. He walked over to André and stared at the wound.

"It looks like an axe cut to me," he said.

Then everyone grew angry at Jean Labadie and his big black dog. They threatened to drive them both out of the parish.

"My friends," said Jean wearily, "I think it is time for this matter to be ended. The truth of it is that I have no big black dog. I never had a big black dog. It was all a joke."

"Aha!" cried André. "Now he is trying to crawl out of the blame. He says he has no big black dog. Yet I have seen it with my own eyes, running around and lifting one paw this way and another paw that way."

"I have seen it, too," cried Madame Villeneuve. "It ran up and growled at me."

"And I."

"And I."

Jean Labadie bowed his head.

"All right, my friends," he said. "There is nothing more I can do about it. I guess that big black dog will eat me out of house and home for the rest of my life."

"You mean you won't make things right about this hand?" demanded André Drouillard.

"What do you want me to do?" asked Jean.

"I will be laid up for a week at least," said André Drouillard, "and right at harvest time. Then, too, there may be a scar. But for two of your plumpest pullets, I am willing to overlook the matter and be friends again."

"That is fair," cried Henri Dupuis.

"It is just," cried the blacksmith.

"A generous proposal," agreed everyone.

"And now we will return to my farm," said Jean Labadie, "and I will give André two of my pullets. But all of you must come. I want witnesses."

A crowd trooped down the road to watch the transaction.

After Jean had given his neighbour two of his best pullets, he commanded the crowd, "Wait!"

He went into the house. When he returned, he was carrying his gun.

"I want witnesses," explained Jean, "because I am going to shoot my big black dog. I want everyone to see this happen."

The crowd murmured and surged. Jean gave a long low whistle toward the henhouse.

"Here comes my big black dog," he pointed. "You can see how he runs to me with his big red tongue hanging out and lifting one paw this way and another paw that way."

Everyone saw the big black dog.

Jean Labadie lifted his gun to his shoulder, pointed it at nothing and pulled the trigger. There was a deafening roar and the gun kicked Jean to the ground. He arose and brushed off his blouse. Madame Villeneuve screamed and Delphine Langlois fainted.

"There," said Jean, brushing away a tear, "it is done. That is the end of my big black dog. Isn't that true?"

And everyone agreed that the dog was gone for good.

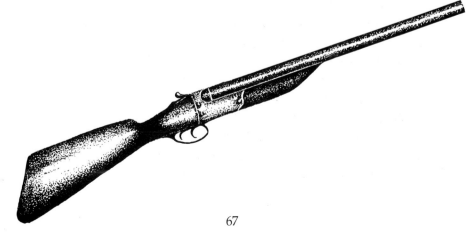

The Shadow-Cage

Philippa Pearce

The little green stoppered bottle had been waiting in the earth a long time for someone to find it. Ned Challis found it. High on his tractor as he ploughed the field, he'd been keeping a look-out, as usual, for whatever might turn up. Several times there had been worked flints; once, one of an enormous size.

Now sunlight glimmering on glass caught his eye. He stopped the tractor, climbed down, picked the bottle from the earth. He could tell at once that it wasn't all that old. Not as old as the flints that he'd taken to the museum in Castleford. Not as old as a coin he had once found, with the head of a Roman emperor on it. Not very old; but old.

Perhaps just useless old . . .

He held the bottle in the palm of his hand and thought of throwing it away. The lip of it was chipped badly, and the stopper of cork or wood had sunk into the neck. With his fingernail he tried to move it. The stopper had hardened into stone, and stuck there. Probably no one would ever get it out now without breaking the bottle. But then, why should anyone want to unstopper the bottle? It was empty, or as good as empty. The bottom of the inside of the bottle was dirtied with something blackish and scaly that also clung a little to the sides.

He wanted to throw the bottle away, but he didn't. He held it in one hand while the fingers of the other cleaned the remaining earth from the outside. When he had cleaned it, he didn't fancy the bottle any more than before; but he dropped it into his pocket. Then he climbed the tractor and started off again.

At that time the sun was high in the sky, and the tractor was working on Whistlers' Hill, which is part of Belper's Farm, fifty yards below Burnt House. As the tractor moved on again, the gulls followed again, rising and falling in their flights, wheeling over the disturbed earth, looking for live things, for food; for good things.

That evening, at tea, Ned Challis brought the bottle out and set it on the table by the loaf of bread. His wife looked at it suspiciously: "Another of your dirty old things for that museum?"

Ned said: "It's not museum-stuff. Lisa can have it to take to school. I don't want it."

Mrs Challis pursed her lips, moved the loaf further away from the bottle, and went to refill the teapot.

Lisa took the bottle in her hand. "Where'd you get it, Dad?"

"Whistlers' Hill. Just below Burnt House." He frowned suddenly as he spoke, as if he had remembered something.

"What's it got inside?"

"Nothing. And if you try getting the stopper out, that'll break."

So Lisa didn't try. Next morning she took it to school; but she didn't show it to anyone. Only her cousin Kevin saw it, and that was before school and by accident. He always called for Lisa on his way to school — there was no other company on that country road — and he saw her pick up the bottle from the table, where her mother had left it the night before, and put it into her anorak pocket.

"What was that?" asked Kevin.

"You saw. A little old bottle."

"Let's see it again — properly." Kevin was younger than Lisa, and she sometimes indulged him; so she took the bottle out and let him hold it.

At once he tried the stopper.

"Don't," said Lisa. "You'll only break it."

"What's inside?"

"Nothing. Dad found it on Whistlers'. "

"It's not very nice, is it?"

"What do you mean, 'Not very nice'?"

"I don't know. But let me keep it for a bit. Please, Lisa."

On principle Lisa now decided not to give in. "Certainly not. Give it back."

He did, reluctantly. "Let me have it just for today, at school. Please."

"No."

"I'll give you something if you'll let me have it. I'll not let anyone else touch it; I'll not let them see it. I'll keep it safe. Just for today."

"You'd only break it. No. What could you give me, anyway?"

"My week's pocket-money."

"No. I've said no and I mean no, young Kev."

"I'd give you that little china dog you like."

"The one with the china kennel?"

"Yes."

"The china dog with the china kennel — you'd give me both?"

"Yes."

"Only for half the day, then," said Lisa. "I'll let you have it after school-dinner — look out for me in the playground. Give it back at the end of school. Without fail. And you be careful with it."

So the bottle travelled to school in Lisa's anorak pocket, where it bided its time all morning. After school-dinner

Lisa met Kevin in the playground and they withdrew together to a corner which was well away from the crowded climbing-frame and the infants' sandpit and the rest. Lisa handed the bottle over. "At the end of school, mind, without fail. And if we miss each other then," — for Lisa, being in a higher class, came out of school slightly later than Kevin — "then you must drop it in at ours as you pass. Promise."

"Promise."

They parted. Kevin put the bottle into his pocket. He didn't know why he'd wanted the bottle, but he had. Lots of things were like that. You needed them for a bit; and then you didn't need them any longer.

He had needed this little bottle very much.

He left Lisa and went over to the climbing-frame, where his friends already were. He had set his foot on a rung when he thought suddenly how easy it would be for the glass bottle in his trouser pocket to be smashed against the metal framework. He stepped down again and went over to the fence that separated the playground from the farmland beyond. Tall tussocks of grass grew along it, coming through from the open fields and fringing the very edge of the asphalt. He looked round: Lisa had already gone in, and no one else was watching. He put his hand into his pocket and took it out again with the bottle concealed in the fist. He stooped as if to examine an insect on a tussock, and slipped his hand into the middle of it and left the bottle there, well hidden.

He straightened up and glanced around. Since no one was looking in his direction, his action had been unobserved; the bottle would be safe. He ran back to the climbing-frame and began to climb, jostling and shouting and laughing, as he and his friends always did. He forgot the bottle.

He forgot the bottle completely.

It was very odd, considering what a fuss he had made about the bottle, that he should have forgotten it; but he did. When the bell rang for the end of playtime, he ran straight in. He did not think of the bottle then, or later. At the end of afternoon school, he did not remember it; and he happened not to see Lisa, who would surely have reminded him.

Only when he was nearly home, and passing the Challises' house, he remembered. He had faithfully promised — and had really meant to keep his promise. But he'd broken it, and left the bottle behind. If he turned and went back to school now, he would meet Lisa, and she would have to be told . . . By the time he got back to the school playground, all his friends would have gone home: the caretaker would be there, and perhaps a late teacher or two, and they'd all want to know what he was up to. And when he'd got the bottle and dropped it in at the Challises', Lisa would scold him all over again. And when he got home at last, he would be very late for his tea, and his mother would be angry.

As he stood by the Challises' gate, thinking, it seemed best, since he had messed things up anyway, to go straight home and leave the bottle to the next day. So he went home.

He worried about the bottle for the rest of the day, without having the time or the quiet to think about it very clearly. He knew that Lisa would assume he had just forgotten to leave it at her house on the way home. He half expected her to turn up after tea, to claim it; but she didn't. She would have been angry enough about his having forgotten to leave it; but what about her anger tomorrow on the way to school, when she found that he had forgotten it altogether — abandoned it in the open playground? He thought of hurrying straight past her house in the morning; but he would never manage it. She would be on the look-out.

He saw that he had made the wrong decision earlier. He ought, at all costs, to have gone back to the playground to get the bottle.

He went to bed, still worrying. He fell asleep, and his worry went on, making his dreaming unpleasant in a nagging way. He must be quick, his dreams seemed to nag. *Be quick . . .*

Suddenly he was wide awake. It was very late. The sound of the television being switched off must have woken him. Quietness. He listened to the rest of his family going to bed. They went to bed and to sleep. Silence. They were all asleep now, except for him. He couldn't sleep.

Then, as abruptly as if someone had lifted the top of his head like a lid and popped the idea in, he saw that this time — almost the middle of the night — was the perfect time for him to fetch the bottle. He knew by heart the roads between home and school; he would not be afraid. He would have plenty of time. When he reached the school, the gate to the playground would be shut, but it was not high: in the past, by daylight, he and his friends had often climbed it. He would go into the playground, find the correct tussock of grass, get the bottle, bring it back, and have it ready to give to Lisa on the way to school in the morning. She would be angry, but only moderately angry. She would never know the whole truth.

He got up and dressed quickly and quietly. He began to look for a pocket-torch, but gave up when he realised that would mean opening and shutting drawers and cupboards. Anyway, there was a moon tonight, and he knew his way, and he knew the school playground. He couldn't go wrong.

He let himself out of the house, leaving the door on the latch for his return. He looked at his watch: between a quarter and half past eleven — not as late as he had thought. All the same, he set off almost at a run, but had to settle down into a steady trot. His trotting footsteps on the road sounded clearly in the night quiet. But who was there to hear?

He neared the Challises' house. He drew level with it.

Ned Challis heard. Usually nothing woke him before the alarm-clock in the morning; but tonight footsteps woke him. Who, at this hour — he lifted the back of his wrist towards his face, so that the time glimmered at him — who, at nearly twenty-five to twelve, could be hurrying along that road on foot? When the footsteps had almost gone — when it was already perhaps too late he sprang out of bed and over to the window.

His wife woke. "What's up, then, Ned?"

"Just somebody. I wondered who."

"Oh, come back to bed!"

Ned Challis went back to bed; but almost at once got out again.

"Ned! What is it now?"

"I just thought I'd have a look at Lisa."

At once Mrs Challis was wide awake. "What's wrong with Lisa?"

"Nothing." He went to listen at Lisa's door — listen to the regular, healthy breathing of her sleep. He came back. "Nothing. Lisa's all right."

"For heaven's sake! Why shouldn't she be?"

"Well, who was it walking out there? Hurrying."

"Oh, go to sleep!"

"Yes," He lay down again, drew the bedclothes round

him, lay still. But his eyes remained open.

Out in the night, Kevin left the road on which the Challises lived and came into the more important one that would take him into the village. He heard the rumble of a lorry coming up behind him. For safety he drew right into a gateway and waited. The lorry came past at a steady pace, headlights on. For a few seconds he saw the driver and his mate sitting up in the cab, intent on the road ahead. He had not wanted to be noticed by them, but, when they had gone, he felt lonely.

He went on into the village, its houses lightless, its streets deserted. By the entrance to the school driveway, he stopped to make sure he was unobserved. Nobody. Nothing — not even a cat. There was no sound of any vehicle now; but in the distance he heard a dog barking, and then another answered it. A little owl cried and cried for company or for sport. Then that, too, stopped.

He turned into the driveway to the school, and there was the gate to the playground. He looked over it, into the playground. Moonlight showed him everything: the expanse of asphalt, the sandpit, the big climbing-frame, and — at the far end — the fence with the tussocks of grass growing blackly along it. It was all familiar, and yet strange because of the emptiness and the whitening of moonlight and the shadows cast like solid things. The climbing-frame reared high into the air, and on the ground stretched the black criss-cross of its shadows like the bars of a cage.

But he had not come all this way to be halted by moonshine and insubstantial shadows. In a businesslike way he climbed the gate and crossed the playground to the fence. He wondered whether he would find the right tussock easily, but he did. His fingers closed on the bottle: it was waiting for him.

At that moment, in the Challises' house, as they lay side by side in bed, Mrs Challis said to her husband: "You're still awake, aren't you?"

"Yes."

"What is it?"

"Nothing."

Mrs Challis sighed.

"All right, then," said Ned Challis. "It's this. That bottle I gave Lisa — that little old bottle that I gave Lisa yesterday — "

"What about it?"

"I found it by Burnt House."

Mrs Challis drew in her breath sharply. Then she said, "That may mean nothing." Then, "How near was it?"

"Near enough." After a pause: "I ought never to have given it to Lisa. I never thought. But Lisa's all right, anyway."

"But, Ned, don't you know what Lisa did with that bottle?"

"What?"

"Lent it to Kevin to have at school. And, according to her, he didn't return it when he should have done, on the way home. Didn't you hear her going on and on about it?"

"Kevin . . ." For the third time that night Ned Challis was getting out of bed, this time putting on his trousers, fumbling for his shoes. "Somebody went up the road in a hurry. You know — I looked out. I couldn't see properly, but it was somebody small. It could have been a child. It could have been Lisa, but it wasn't. It could well have been Kevin . . ."

"Shouldn't you go to their house first, Ned — find out whether Kevin is there or not? Make sure. You're not sure."

"I'm not sure. But, if I wait to make sure, I may be too

late."

Mrs Challis did not say, "Too late for what?" She did not argue.

Ned Challis dressed and went down. As he let himself out of the house to get his bicycle from the shed, the church clock began to strike the hour, the sound reaching him distantly across the intervening fields. He checked with his watch: midnight.

In the village, in the school playground, the striking of midnight sounded clangorously close. Kevin stood with the bottle held in the palm of his hand, waiting for the clock to stop striking — waiting as if for something to follow.

After the last stroke of midnight, there was silence, but Kevin still stood waiting and listening. A car or lorry passed the entrance of the school drive: he heard it distinctly; yet it was oddly faint, too. He couldn't place the oddness of it. It had sounded much further away than it should have done — less really there.

He gripped the bottle and went on listening, as if for some particular sound. The minutes passed. The same dog barked at the same dog, bark and reply — far, unreally far away. The little owl called; from another world, it might have been.

He was gripping the bottle so tightly now that his hand was sweating. He felt his skin begin to prickle with sweat at the back of his neck and under his arms.

Then there was a whistle from across the fields, distantly. It should have been an unexpected sound, just after midnight; but it did not startle him. It did set him off across the playground, however. Too late he wanted to get away. He had to go past the climbing-frame, whose cagework of shadows now stretched more largely than the frame itself. He saw the bars of shadow as he

77

approached; he actually hesitated; and then, like a fool, he stepped inside the cage of shadows.

Ned Challis, on his bicycle, had reached the junction of the by-road with the road that — in one direction — led to the village. In the other it led deeper into the country. Which way? He dismounted. He had to choose the right way — to follow Kevin.

Thinking of Whistlers' Hill, he turned the front wheel of his bicycle away from the village and set off again. But now, with his back to the village, going away from the village, he felt a kind of weariness and despair. A memory of childhood came into his mind: a game he had played in childhood: something hidden for him to find, and if he turned in the wrong direction to search, all the voices whispered to him, "Cold — cold!" Now, with the village receding behind him, he recognized what he felt: cold . . . cold . . .

Without getting off his bicycle, he wheeled round and began to pedal hard in the direction of the village.

In the playground, there was no pressing hurry for Kevin any more. He did not press against the bars of his cage to get out. Even when clouds cut off the moonlight and the shadows melted into general darkness — even when the shadow-cage was no longer visible to the eye, he stood there; then crouched there, in a corner of the cage, as befitted a prisoner.

The church clock struck the quarter.

The whistlers were in no hurry. The first whistle had come from right across the fields. Then there was a long pause. Then the sound was repeated, equally distantly, from the direction of the river bridges. Later still, another whistle from the direction of the railway line, or somewhere near it.

He lay in his cage, cramped by the bars, listening. He

did not know he was thinking, but suddenly it came to him: Whistlers' Hill. He and Lisa and the others had always supposed that the hill had belonged to a family called Whistler, as Challises' house belonged to the Challis family. But that was not how the hill had got its name — he saw that now. No, indeed not.

Whistler answered whistler at long intervals, like the sentries of a besieging army. There was no moving in as yet.

The church clock had struck the quarter as Ned Challis entered the village and cycled past the entrance to the school. He cycled as far as the Recreation Ground, perhaps because that was where Kevin would have gone in the daytime. He cycled bumpily round the Ground: no Kevin.

He began to cycle back the way he had come, as though he had given up altogether and were going home. He cycled slowly. He passed the entrance to the school again.

In this direction, he was leaving the village. He was cycling so slowly that the front wheel of his bicycle wobbled desperately; the light from his dynamo was dim. He put a foot down and stopped. Motionless, he listened. There was nothing to hear, unless — yes, the faintest ghost of a sound, high pitched, prolonged for seconds, remote as from another world. Like a coward — and Ned Challis was no coward — he tried to persuade himself that he had imagined the sound; yet he knew he had not. It came from another direction now: very faint, yet penetrating, so that his skin crinkled to hear it. Again it came, from yet another quarter.

He wheeled his bicycle back to the entrance to the school and left it there. He knew he must be very close. He walked up to the playground gate and peered over it.

79

But the moon was obscured by cloud: he could see nothing. He listened, waited for the moon to sail free.

In the playground Kevin had managed to get up, first on his hands and knees, then upright. He was very much afraid, but he had to be standing to meet whatever it was.

For the whistlers had begun to close in slowly, surely: converging on the school, on the school playground, on the cage of shadows. On him.

For some time now cloud-masses had obscured the moon. He could see nothing; but he felt the whistlers' presence. Their signals came more often, and always closer. Closer. Very close.

Suddenly the moon sailed free.

In the sudden moonlight Ned Challis saw clear across the playground to where Kevin stood against the climbing-frame, with his hands writhing together in front of him.

In the sudden moonlight Kevin did not see his uncle. Between him and the playground gate, and all round him, air was thickening into darkness. Frantically he tried to undo his fingers, that held the little bottle, so that he could throw it from him. But he could not. He held the bottle; the bottle held him.

The darkness was closing in on him. The darkness was about to take him; had surely got him.

Kevin shrieked.

Ned Challis shouted: "I'm here!" and was over the gate and across the playground and with his arms round the boy: *"I've got you."*

There was a tinkle as something fell from between Kevin's opened fingers: the little bottle fell and rolled to the middle of the playground. It lay there, very insignificant-looking.

Kevin was whimpering and shaking, but he could

move of his own accord. Ned Challis helped him over the gate and to the bicycle.

"Do you think you could sit on the bar, Kev? Could you manage that?"

"Yes." He could barely speak.

Ned Challis hesitated, thinking of the bottle which had chosen to come to rest in the very centre of the playground, where the first child tomorrow would see it, pick it up.

He went back and picked the bottle up. Wherever he threw it, someone might find it. He might smash it and grind the pieces underfoot; but he was not sure he dared to do that.

Anyway, he was not going to hold it in his hand longer than he strictly must. He put it into his pocket, and then, when he got back to Kevin and the bicycle, he slipped it into the saddlebag.

He rode Kevin home on the crossbar of his bicycle. At the Challises' front gate Mrs Challis was waiting, with the dog for company. She just said: "He all right then?"

"Ah."

"I'll make a cup of tea while you take him home."

At his own front door, Kevin said: "I left the door on the latch. I can get in. I'm all right. I'd rather — I'd rather — "

"Less spoken of, the better," said his uncle. "You go to bed. Nothing to be afraid of now."

He waited until Kevin was inside the house and he heard the latch click into place. Then he rode back to his wife, his cup of tea, and consideration of the problem that lay in his saddlebag.

After he had told his wife everything, and they had discussed possibilities, Ned Challis said thoughtfully: "I might take it to the museum, after all. Safest place for it would be inside a glass case there."

"But you said they wouldn't want it."

"Perhaps they would, if I told them where I found it and a bit — only a bit — about Burnt House . . ."

"You do that, then."

Ned Challis stood up and yawned with a finality that said, Bed.

"But don't you go thinking you've solved all your problems by taking that bottle to Castleford, Ned. Not by a long chalk."

"No?"

"Lisa. She reckons she owns that bottle."

"I'll deal with Lisa tomorrow."

"Today, by the clock."

Ned Challis gave a groan that turned into another yawn. "Bed first," he said; "then Lisa." They went to bed not long before the dawn.

The next day and for days after that, Lisa was furiously angry with her father. He had as good as stolen her bottle, she said, and now he refused to give it back, to let her see it, even to tell her what he had done with it. She was less angry with Kevin. (She did not know, of course, the circumstances of the bottle's passing from Kevin to her father.)

Kevin kept out of Lisa's way, and even more carefully kept out of his uncle's. He wanted no private conversation.

One Saturday Kevin was having tea at the Challises', because he had been particularly invited. He sat with Lisa and Mrs Challis. Ned had gone to Castleford, and came in late. He joined them at the tea-table in evident good spirits. From his pocket he brought out a small cardboard box, which he placed in the centre of the table, by the Saturday cake. His wife was staring at him: before he spoke, he gave her the slightest nod of reassurance. "The museum didn't want to keep that little old glass bottle, after all," he said.

Both the children gave a cry: Kevin started up with such a violent backward movement that his chair clattered to the floor behind him; Lisa leant forward, her fingers clawing towards the box.

"No!" Ned Challis said. To Lisa he added: "There it stays, girl, till *I* say." To Kevin: "Calm down. Sit up at the table again and listen to me." Kevin picked his chair up and sat down again, resting his elbows on the table, so that his hands supported his head.

"Now," said Ned Challis, "you two know so much that it's probably better you should know more. That little old bottle came from Whistlers' Hill, below Burnt House — well, you know that. Burnt House is only a ruin now — elder bushes growing inside as well as out; but once it was a cottage that someone lived in. Your mother's granny remembered the last one to live there."

"No, Ned," said Mrs Challis, "it was my great-granny remembered."

"Anyway," said Ned Challis, "it was so long ago that Victoria was the Queen, that's certain. And an old woman lived alone in that cottage. There were stories about her."

"Was she a witch?" breathed Lisa.

"So they said. They said she went out on the hillside at night — "

"At the full of the moon," said Mrs Challis.

"They said she dug up roots and searched out plants and toadstools and things. They said she caught rats and toads and even bats. They said she made ointments and powders and weird brews. And they said she used what she made to cast spells and call up spirits."

"Spirits from Hell, my great-granny said. Real bad 'uns."

"So people said, in the village. Only the parson scoffed at the whole idea. Said he'd called often and been shown over the cottage and seen nothing out of the ordinary — none of the jars and bottles of stuff that she was supposed to have for her witchcraft. He said she was just a poor cranky old woman; that was all.

"Well, she grew older and older and crankier and crankier, and one day she died. Her body lay in its coffin in the cottage, and the parson was going to bury her next day in the churchyard.

"The night before she was to have been buried, someone went up from the village — "

"Someone!" said Mrs Challis scornfully. "Tell them the whole truth, Ned, if you're telling the story at all. Half the village went up, with lanterns — men, women, and children. Go on, Ned."

"The cottage was thatched, and they began to pull swatches of straw away and take it into the cottage and strew it round and heap it up under the coffin. They were going to fire it all.

"They were pulling the straw on the downhill side of the cottage when suddenly a great piece of thatch came away and out came tumbling a whole lot of things that the old woman must have kept hidden there. People did hide things in thatches, in those days."

"Her savings?" asked Lisa.

"No. A lot of jars and little bottles, all stoppered or sealed, neat and nice. With stuff inside."

There was a silence at the tea-table. Then Lisa said: "That proved it: she was a witch."

"Well, no, it only proved she *thought* she was a witch. That was what the parson said afterwards — and whew! was he mad when he knew about that night."

Mrs Challis said: "He gave it 'em red hot from the pulpit

the next Sunday. He said that once upon a time poor old deluded creatures like her had been burnt alive for no reason at all, and the village ought to be ashamed of having burnt her dead."

Lisa went back to the story of the night itself. "What did they do with what came out of the thatch?"

"Bundled it inside the cottage among the straw, and fired it all. The cottage burnt like a beacon that night, they say. Before cockcrow, everything had been burnt to ashes. That's the end of the story."

"Except for my little bottle," said Lisa. "That came out of the thatch, but it didn't get picked up. It rolled downhill, or someone kicked it."

"That's about it," Ned agreed.

Lisa stretched her hand again to the cardboard box, and this time he did not prevent her. But he said: "Don't be surprised, Lisa. It's different."

She paused. "A different bottle?"

"The same bottle, but — well you'll see."

Lisa opened the box, lifted the packaging of cotton wool, took the bottle out. It was the same bottle, but the stopper had gone, and it was empty and clean — so clean that it shone greenly. Innocence shone from it.

"You said the stopper would never come out," Lisa said slowly.

"They forced it by suction. The museum chap wanted to know what was inside, so he got the hospital lab to take a look — he has a friend there. It was easy for them."

Mrs Challis said: "That would make a pretty vase, Lisa. For tiny flowers." She coaxed Lisa to go out to pick a posy from the garden; she herself took the bottle away to fill it with water.

Ned Challis and Kevin faced each other across the table. Kevin said: "What was in it?"

Ned Challis said: "A trace of this, a trace of that, the hospital said. One thing more than anything else."

"Yes?"

"Blood. Human blood."

Lisa came back with her flowers; Mrs Challis came back with the bottle filled with water. When the flowers had been put in, it looked a pretty thing.

"My witch-bottle," said Lisa contentedly. "What was she called — the old woman that thought she was a witch?"

Her father shook his head; her mother thought: "Madge — or was it Maggy —?"

"Maggy Whistler's bottle, then," said Lisa.

"Oh, no," said Mrs Challis. "She was Maggy — or Madge — Dawson. I remember my granny saying so. Dawson."

"Then why's it called Whistlers' Hill?"

"I'm not sure," said Mrs Challis uneasily. "I mean, I don't think anyone knows for certain."

But Ned Challis, looking at Kevin's face, knew that he knew for certain.

The Snail Collector

Michael Baldwin

One day I sat talking to myself in the garden. I had two armies, one in the pile of stones and one in the grass. I could see the army in the grass advancing, and my lips were booming the guns.

"Got any snails?" said a voice.

I looked up. A clean boy, with a jacket on, stood on top of the wall that was the edge of the town. He was very smart for the alley. Generally I did not answer people from there. But he looked all right. I was not supposed to speak to boys without jackets; nor to the family without shoes down the road.

"Snails?" I asked. Then, as he climbed over the wall, "Be careful of the rhubarb."

"Rhubarb! My father's got fifty cabbages!" he kicked round the plants. "Yes: I can see you've got plenty. Half a mo: I'll be back with my bucket." And he was gone again. I heard his footsteps slap down the alley.

I went back to my battle. There was smoke all over the garden.

"Where are they, then?"

I looked up, feeling cross. He was already climbing the wall, with a creaking bucket. He wore sandals. I had always wanted sandals.

"Haven't you got me any?"

I went on with my game.

After a time I grew intrigued to hear the bucket creaking

round and round the garden. He kept on talking to himself too, saying things like: "Yes, I thought so . . . I thought so . . . there's another one . . . that's worth a pretty penny . . .", just like a grown-up.

I went and watched him. He had a pile of snails in the bucket. "That's stealing," I said.

"What – snails? People kill snails."

"That's what my dad does," I said. "And Boss, and Nan. And Aunt Rene!" And I killed one with a stone.

"Spoil sport," he said.

"Who's that, Michael?" asked my grandmother's voice from the back door.

The boy got ready to run.

"Only me, Nan," I called out. The garden was very quiet. It was my first big lie.

"Come on then," he said. "Let's go." And he went over the wall.

I caught at the big sharp flints and struggled after him. It was hard to get up; but the alley was near on the other side. Wully the cat was coming along with a dead bird in his mouth like a ripe plum. I always found myself seeing things. We ran down the alley.

The world was much larger, flint walls, and mud, and edges of grass, as we ran past all the back gardens in a row. We came out at the greengrocers where Nan took me to buy vegetables. The boy ran across the road. "Come on," he called.

I had never crossed a road before, but I went, wondering which was the way home. He opened a gate by a shop and we ran down a path. "Here they are," he said.

There were two tea-chests in the garden, joined by pieces of wood. He lifted the lids of the tea-chests, and I saw them — hundreds of snails, hundreds, eyes on horns, eyes going into horns, bodies going into houses, shells of all sorts of colours, black, brown, grey, mottled ones and striped ones. They were sticking to the floor, the walls, the lid, and to one another, in great bunches like conkers. They were wonderful.

He put back the lids, and then took a snail from his pocket. It was snow-white. "Whitewash," he explained. Then he brought out a handful of pink ones. I gasped. "The house," he said. I saw the house was painted pink, and that there were ladders and pots by the wall, and I understood him.

"You and me," he said.

"When?" I asked.

"Always," he said. Then he picked up the bucket and called out "C'mon." We went carefully through his father's fifty cabbages, leaf by leaf. We turned wood by the wall; we kicked over bricks and stones. Everywhere we went there were snails. We talked to them, kissed their shells, and put them in the bucket.

"C'mon," he said again. And we went out of the gate.

Once more I crossed the road, and once more went up the alley, which was now full of people. They called their words, but we had things to do. Over the wall we went, and into the rhubarb. The garden was wet and smelled of elderberry and cat.

"Where've you been?" called Nan.

"Hiding," I lied.

She came out and hooded her eyes in the sun. It was too much for them and she went in. We were poachers and the great adventure of the snails went on.

It went on for weeks. We collected them and their babies by the bucketful. His father would kill them among the weeds, so they were our secret. We prowled around one another's houses with them in our hands and pushed them down the backs of chairs so that they would be comfortable. Sometimes we put them in the salad for a laugh, so the women would scream, and we could eat all of the family's lettuce. Sometimes we put them in our pockets and sat on them; but we tried to treat them kindly, because we loved them.

One day we raced our snails on the table where his father sold trousers. I had watched through a door while his father stood with a measure round his neck and chalk in his hands, talking to men with creases; I had watched the blinds drawn up and the cloth folded, and his father go in to tea. Then we pulled the table from the shop into the yard, and started our races. The table was leathery green and the snails moved along it unrolling silver slime. We raced them in twos and fours. A face stood at my shoulder.

Then another, breathing over my head.

Then another.

The *boys* had got in!

One put his hand on a snail and pulled it, plop, from the table. It was Beauty!

He held it high in the air while my partner grabbed at it. Then he bent down and scooped its shell in some sand. Beauty bubbled through the sand and the sand wriggled. We grabbed again. He held us off, and the shell snapped between his thumb and finger. He wiped it off on my partner's coat.

We started to cry.

They did not run in a hurry: they jeered until they heard footsteps. Then they walked through the gate and slammed it shut.

His mother stood beside us.

We went on crying: but all she saw was the table covered with lines and the box of snails.

I knew it was the end, even if his father did not find out. She had told us off before, about him wrapping snails in his handkerchief and spoiling the wash. Last night he had taken some to bed with him and rolled on them. It was our last chance.

He went on crying.

He was doing well. His mother was holding his head; and I was wiping the table. Then his dad came out.

She was on our side, but his dad told us off about pockets, and cabbages, and spoiling the garden. It was no use her winking. She did not stop him, even when he said "At once!"

"Get rid of them, *at once*," he said. And they both went in.

My partner stopped crying the minute they went. He kicked at the table. Then he kicked a flowerpot smash against a wall.

"Upstairs," he said.

I looked at him, trying to know what he meant. With his red face I never knew. I did what he said because he seemed to know, to have done things before like my family had.

We picked up the smallest box and took it up through the shop, up the wooden stairs where his father kept shoes and leather.

Up in the attic we tipped them on to the floor. The sticky ones we stuck on the walls.

"I'll know they're here," he said. He kissed one and wrapped it up in some cloth that had the white lines men wear for trousers.

We went downstairs for the other box.

His father's fifty cabbages stood like trees for a battle. We dropped all the snails into the slots of the cabbages and thought of them living there. We had one or two left.

"These are no good," he said.

So we killed them.

When I went home I sat listening to stories, and wanted to say about the snails. But I couldn't. I wanted to do my own story, so I could nod, and hum, and look in the air, and cough by the fire, until they asked what my story was.

Then I should tell them.

The Summer of
the Beautiful White Horse

William Saroyan

One day back there in the good old days when I was nine and the world was full of every imaginable kind of magnificence, and life was still a delightful and mysterious dream, my cousin Mourad, who was considered crazy by everybody who knew him except me, came to my house at four in the morning and woke me up by tapping on the window of my room.

"Aram," he said.

I jumped out of bed and looked out of the window. I couldn't believe what I saw.

It wasn't morning yet, but it was summer and with daybreak not many minutes around the corner of the world it was light enough for me to know I wasn't dreaming.

My cousin Mourad was sitting on a beautiful white horse. I stuck my head out of the window and rubbed my eyes.

"Yes," he said. "It's a horse. You're not dreaming. Make it quick if you want to ride."

I knew my cousin Mourad enjoyed being alive more than anybody else who had ever fallen into the world by mistake, but this was more than even I could believe. In the first place, my earliest memories had been memories of horses and my first longings had been longings to ride.

This was the wonderful part.

In the second place, we were poor.

This was the part that wouldn't permit me to believe what I saw.

We were poor. We had no money. Our whole tribe was poverty-stricken. Every branch of the family was living in the most amazing and comical poverty in the world. Nobody could understand where we ever got money enough to keep us with food in our bellies, not even the old men in the family. Most important of all, though, we were famous for our honesty. We had been famous for our honesty for something like eleven centuries, even when we had been the wealthiest family in what we liked to think was the world. We were proud first, honest next, and after that we believed in right and wrong. None of us would take advantage of anybody in the world, let alone steal.

Consequently, even though I could *see* the horse, so magnificent; even though I could *smell* it, so lovely; even though I could *hear* it breathing, so exciting; I couldn't *believe* the horse had anything to do with my cousin Mourad or with me or with any of the other members of our family, asleep or awake, because I *knew* my cousin Mourad couldn't have *bought* the horse, and if he couldn't have bought it he must have *stolen* it, and I refused to believe he had stolen it.

No member of the family could be a thief.

I stared first at my cousin and then at the horse.

"Let me put on some clothes," I said.

"All right," he said, "but hurry."

I leaped into my clothes.

I jumped down to the yard from the window and leaped up on the horse behind my cousin Mourad. The horse began to trot. The air was new and lovely to breathe. The feel of the horse running was wonderful.

My cousin Mourad who was considered one of the

craziest members of our family began to sing. I mean, he began to roar.

Every family has a crazy streak in it somewhere, and my cousin Mourad was considered the natural descendant of the crazy streak in our tribe.

We rode and my cousin Mourad sang. We let the horse run as long as it felt like running. At last my cousin Mourad said, "Get down. I want to ride alone."

"Will you let me ride alone?" I said.

"That is up to the horse," my cousin said. "Get down."

"The *horse* will let me ride." I said.

"We shall see," he said. "Don't forget that I have a way with a horse."

"Well," I said, "any way you have with a horse, I have also."

I got down and my cousin Mourad kicked his heels into the horse and shouted, "Run". The horse stood on its hind legs, snorted, and burst into a fury of speed that was the loveliest thing I had ever seen. My cousin Mourad raced the horse across a field of dry grass to an irrigation ditch, crossed the ditch on the horse, and five minutes later returned, dripping wet.

The sun was coming up.

"Now it's my turn to ride," I said.

I leaped to the back of the horse and for a moment knew the awfullest fear imaginable. The horse did not move. "Kick into his muscles," my cousin Mourad said. "What are you waiting for? We've got to take him back before everybody in the world is up and about."

I kicked into the muscles of the horse. Once again it reared and snorted. Then it began to run. I didn't know what to do. Instead of running across the field to the irrigation ditch the horse ran down the road to a vineyard where it began to leap over vines. The horse leaped over seven vines before I fell. Then it continued running. My cousin Mourad came running down the road.

"I'm not worried about you," he shouted. "We've got to get that horse. You go this way and I'll go that way. If you come upon him, be kindly. I'll be near." It took us half an hour to find the horse.

"All right," he said, "jump on. The whole world is awake now."

"What will we do now?" I said.

"Well," he said, "we'll either take him back or hide him until tomorrow morning." He didn't sound worried and I knew he'd hide him and not take him back. Not for a while, at any rate.

"Where will we hide him?" I said.

"I know a place," he said.

He walked the horse quietly to the barn of a deserted vineyard. There were some oats and dry alfalfa in the barn. We began walking home.

"It wasn't easy," he said, "to get the horse to behave so nicely. At first it wanted to run wild, but, as I've told you, I have a way with a horse. I can get it to want to do anything *I* want it to do. Horses understand me."

"How do you do it?" I said.

"I have an understanding with a horse," he said.

"Yes, but what sort of an understanding?" I said.

"A simple and honest one," he said.

"Well," I said, "I wish I knew how to reach an understanding like that with a horse."

"You're still a small boy," he said. "When you get to be thirteen you'll know how to do it."

I went home and ate a hearty breakfast. That afternoon my uncle Khosrove came to our house for coffee and cigarettes. He sat in the parlour, sipping and smoking and remembering the old country. Then another visitor arrived, a farmer named John Byro. My mother brought the lonely visitor coffee and tobacco and he rolled a cigarette and sipped and smoked, and then at last, sighing sadly, he said, "My white horse which was stolen last month is still gone. I cannot understand it."

My uncle Khosrove became very irritated and shouted, "It's no harm. What is the loss of a horse? Haven't we all lost the homeland? What is this crying over a horse?"

"That may be all right for you, a city dweller, to say," John Byro said, "but what of my surrey? What good is a surrey without a horse?"

"Pay no attention to it," my uncle Khosrove roared.

"I walked ten miles to get here," John Byro said.

"You have legs," my uncle Khosrove shouted.

"My left leg pains me," the farmer said.

"Pay no attention to it," my uncle Khosrove roared.

"That horse cost me sixty dollars," the farmer said.

"I spit on money," my uncle Khosrove said. He got up and stalked out of the house, slamming the screen door.

My mother explained. "He has a gentle heart," she said. "It is simply that he is homesick and such a large man."

The farmer went away and I ran over to my cousin Mourad's house. He was sitting under a peach-tree, trying to repair the hurt wing of a young robin which could not fly. He was talking to the bird.

"What is it?" he said.

"The farmer, John Byro," I said. "He visited our house. He wants his horse. You've had it a month. I want you to promise not to take it back until I learn to ride."

"It will take you a *year* to learn to ride," my cousin Mourad said.

"We could keep the horse a year," I said. My cousin Mourad leaped to his feet.

"What?" he roared. "Are you inviting a member of the family to steal? The horse must go back to its true owner."

"When?" I said.

"In six months at the latest," he said. He threw the bird into the air. The bird tried hard, almost fell, but at last flew away, high and straight.

Early every morning for two weeks my cousin Mourad and I took the horse out of the barn of the deserted vineyard where we were hiding it and rode it; and every morning the horse, when it was my turn to ride alone, leaped over grape vines and small trees and threw me and ran away. Nevertheless, I hoped in time to learn to ride the way my cousin Mourad rode.

One morning on the way to the deserted vineyard we ran into the farmer John Byro, who was on his way to town.

"Let me do the talking," my cousin Mourad said. "I have a way with farmers."

"Good morning, John Byro," my cousin Mourad said to the farmer.

The farmer studied the horse eagerly.

"Good morning, sons of my friends," he said. "What is the name of your horse?"

"My Heart," my cousin Mourad said in Armenian.

"A lovely name," John Byro said, "for a lovely horse. I could swear it is the horse that was stolen from me many weeks ago. May I look into its mouth?"

"Of course," Mourad said.

The farmer looked into the mouth of the horse.

"Tooth for tooth," he said. "I would swear it *is* my horse if I didn't know your parents. The fame of your family for honesty is well known to me. Yet the horse is the twin of my horse. A suspicious man would believe his eyes instead of his heart. Good day, my young friends."

"Good day, John Byro," my cousin Mourad said.

Early the following morning we took the horse to John Byro's vineyard and put it in the barn. The dogs followed us around without making a sound.

"The dogs," I whispered. "I thought they would bark."

"They would at somebody else," he said. "I have a way with dogs."

My cousin Mourad put his arms around the horse, pressed his nose into the horse's nose, patted it, and then we went away.

That afternoon John Byro came to our house in his surrey and showed my mother the horse that had been stolen and returned.

"I do not know what to think," he said. "The horse is stronger than ever. Better-tempered, too. I thank God."

My uncle Khosrove, who was in the parlour, became irritated and shouted, "Quiet, man, quiet. Your horse has been returned. Pay no attention to it."

The Mixer

P. G. Wodehouse

Looking back, I always consider that my career as a dog proper really started when I was bought for the sum of half a crown by the Shy Man. That event marked the end of my puppyhood. The knowledge that I was worth actual cash to somebody filled me with a sense of new responsibilities. It sobered me. Besides, it was only after that half-crown changed hands that I went out into the great world; and, however interesting life may be in an East End public-house, it is only when you go out into the world that you really broaden your mind and begin to see things.

Within its limitations, my life had been singularly full and vivid. I was born, as I say, in a public-house in the East End, and however lacking a public-house may be in refinement and the true culture, it certainly provides plenty of excitement. Before I was six weeks old, I had upset three policemen by getting between their legs when they came round to the side door, thinking they had heard suspicious noises; and I can still recall the interesting sensation of being chased seventeen times round the yard with a broom-handle after a well-planned and completely successful raid on the larder. These and other happenings of a like nature soothed for the moment but could not cure the restlessness which has always been so marked a trait in my character. I have always been restless, unable to settle down in one place and anxious to get on to the next thing. This may be due to a gipsy strain in my ancestry — one of my uncles travelled with a circus — or it may be the Artistic Temperament, acquired from a grandfather who, before dying of a surfeit of paste in the property-room of the Bristol Coliseum, which he was visiting in the course of a professional tour, had an established reputation on the music-hall as one of Professor Pond's Performing Poodles.

I owe the fullness and variety of my life to this restlessness of mine, for I have repeatedly left comfortable homes in order to follow some perfect stranger who looked as if he were on his way to somewhere interesting. Sometimes I think I must have cat blood in me.

The Shy Man came into our yard one afternoon in April, while I was sleeping with mother in the sun on an old sweater which we had borrowed from Fred, one of the barmen. I heard mother growl, but I didn't take any notice. Mother is what they call a good watchdog, and she growls at everybody except master. At first, when she used to do it, I would get up and bark my head off, but not now. Life's too short to bark at everybody who comes into our yard. It is behind the public-house, and they keep empty bottles and things there, so people are always coming and going.

Besides, I was tired. I had had a very busy morning, helping the men bring in a lot of cases of beer, and running into the saloon to talk to Fred and generally looking after things. So I was just dozing off again, when I heard a voice say, "Well, he's ugly enough!" Then I knew that they were talking about me.

I have never disguised it from myself, and nobody has ever disguised it from me, that I am not a handsome dog. Even mother never thought me beautiful. She was no

Gladys Cooper herself, but she never hesitated to criticise my appearance. In fact, I have yet to meet anyone who did. The first thing strangers say about me is, "What an ugly dog!"

I don't know what I am. I have a bulldog kind of a face, but the rest of me is terrier. I have a long tail which sticks straight up in the air. My hair is wiry. My eyes are brown. I am jet black, with a white chest. I once overheard Fred saying that I was a Gorgonzola cheese-hound, and I have generally found Fred reliable in his statements.

When I found that I was under discussion, I opened my eyes. Master was standing there, looking down at me, and by his side the man who had just said I was ugly enough. The man was a thin man, about the age of a barman and smaller than a policeman. He had patched brown shoes and black trousers.

"But he's got a sweet nature," said master.

This was true, luckily for me. Mother always said, "A dog without influence or private means, if he is to make his way in the world, must have either good looks or amiability." But, according to her, I overdid it. "A dog," she used to say, "can have a good heart, without chumming with every Tom, Dick, and Harry he meets. Your behaviour is sometimes quite un-doglike." Mother prided herself on being a one-man dog. She kept herself to herself, and wouldn't kiss anybody except master — not even Fred.

Now, I'm a mixer. I can't help it. It's my nature. I like men. I like the taste of their boots, the smell of their legs, and the sound of their voices. It may be weak of me, but a man has only to speak to me and a sort of thrill goes right down my spine and sets my tail wagging.

I wagged it now. The man looked at me rather distantly. He didn't pat me. I suspected — what I afterwards found to be the case — that he was shy, so I jumped up at him to put him at his ease. Mother growled again. I felt that she did not approve.

"Why, he's took quite a fancy to you already," said master.

The man didn't say a word. He seemed to be brooding on something. He was one of those silent men. He reminded me of Joe, the old dog down the street at the grocer's shop, who lies at the door all day, blinking and not speaking to anybody.

Master began to talk about me. It surprised me, the way he praised me. I hadn't a suspicion he admired me so much. From what he said you would have thought I had won prizes and ribbons at the Crystal Palace. But the man didn't seem to be impressed. He kept on saying nothing.

When master had finished telling him what a wonderful dog I was till I blushed, the man spoke.

"Less of it," he said. "Half a crown is my bid, and if he was an angel from on high you couldn't get another ha'penny out of me. What about it?"

A thrill went down my spine and out at my tail, for of course I saw now what was happening. The man wanted to buy me and take me away. I looked at master hopefully.

"He's more like a son to me than a dog," said master, sort of wistful.

"It's his face that makes you feel that way," said the man, unsympathetically. "If you had a son that's just how he would look. Half a crown is my offer, and I'm in a hurry."

"All right," said master, with a sigh, "though it's giving him away, a valuable dog like that. Where's your half-crown?"

The man got a bit of rope and tied it round my neck.

I could hear mother barking advice and telling me to be a credit to the family, but I was too excited to listen.

"Goodbye mother," I said. "Goodbye, master. Goodbye Fred. Goodbye everybody. I'm off to see life. The Shy Man has bought me for half a crown. Wow!"

I kept running round in circles and shouting, till the man gave me a kick and told me to stop it.

So I did.

I don't know where we went, but it was a long way. I had never been off our street before in my life and I didn't know the whole world was half as big as that. We walked on and on, the man jerking at my rope whenever I wanted to stop and look at anything. He wouldn't even let me pass the time of the day with dogs we met.

When we had gone about a hundred miles and were just going to turn in at a dark doorway, a policeman suddenly stopped the man. I could feel by the way the man pulled at my rope and tried to hurry on that he didn't want to speak to the policeman. The more I saw of the man, the more I saw how shy he was.

"Hi!" said the policeman, and we had to stop.

"I've got a message for you, old pal," said the policeman. "It's from the Board of Health. They told me to tell you you needed a change of air. See?"

"All right!" said the man.

"And take it as soon as you like. Else you'll find you'll get it given you. See?"

I looked at the man with a good deal of respect. He was evidently someone important, if they worried so about his health.

"I'm going down to the country tonight," said the man.

The policeman seemed pleased.

"That's a bit of luck for the country," he said. "Don't go changing your mind."

And we walked on, and went in at the dark doorway, and climbed about a million stairs and went into a room that smelt of rats. The man sat down and swore a little, and I sat and looked at him.

Presently I couldn't keep it in any longer.

"Do we live here?" I said. "Is it true we're going to the country? Wasn't that policeman a good sort? Don't you like policemen? I knew lots of policemen at the public-house. Are there any other dogs here? What is there for dinner? What's in that cupboard? When are you going to take me out for another run? May I go out and see if I can find a cat?"

"Stop that yelping," he said.

"When we go to the country, where shall we live? Are you going to be caretaker at a house? Fred's father is a caretaker at a big house in Kent. I've heard Fred talk about it. You didn't meet Fred when you came to the public-house, did you? You would like Fred. I like Fred. Mother likes Fred. We all like Fred."

I was going to tell him a lot more about Fred, who had always been one of my warmest friends, when he suddenly got hold of a stick and walloped me with it.

"You keep quiet when you're told," he said.

He really was the shyest man I had ever met. It seemed to hurt him to be spoken to. However, he was the boss, and I had to humour him, so I didn't say any more.

We went down to the country that night, just as the man had told the policeman we would. I was all worked up, for I had heard so much about the country from Fred that I had always wanted to go there. Fred used to go off on a motor-bicycle sometimes to spend the night with his father in Kent, and once he brought back a squirrel with him, which I thought was for me to eat, but mother said no. "The first thing a dog has to learn," mother used often to say, "is that the whole world wasn't created for him to eat."

It was quite dark when we got to the country, but the man seemed to know where to go. He pulled at my rope, and we began to walk along a road with no people in it at all. We walked on and on, but it was all so new to me that I forgot how tired I was. I could feel my mind broadening with every step I took.

Every now and then we would pass a very big house, which looked as if it was empty, but I knew that there was a caretaker inside, because of Fred's father. These big houses belong to very rich people, but they don't want to live in them till the summer, so they put in caretakers, and the caretakers have a dog to keep off burglars. I wondered if that was what I had been brought here for.

"Are you going to be a caretaker?" I asked the man.

"Shut up," he said.

So I shut up.

After we had been walking a long time, we came to a cottage. A man came out. My man seemed to know him, for he called him Bill. I was quite surprised to see the man was not at all shy with Bill. They seemed very friendly.

"Is that him?" said Bill, looking at me.

"Bought him this afternoon," said the man.

"Well," said Bill, "he's ugly enough. He looks fierce. If you want a dog, he's the sort of dog you want. But what do you want one for? It seems to me it's a lot of trouble to take, when there's no need of any trouble at all. Why not do what I've always wanted to do? What's wrong with just fixing the dog, same as it's always done, and walking in and helping yourself?"

"I'll tell you what's wrong," said the man. "To start with, you can't get at the dog and fix him except by day, when they let him out. At night he's shut up inside the house. And suppose you do fix him during the day, what happens then? Either the bloke gets another before night, or else he sits up all night with a gun. It isn't like as if these blokes was ordinary blokes. They're down here to look after the house. That's their job, and they don't take any chances."

It was the longest speech I had ever heard the man make, and it seemed to impress Bill. He was quite humble.

"I didn't think of that," he said. "We'd best start in to train this tyke at once."

Mother often used to say, when I went on about wanting to go out into the world and see life, "You'll be sorry when you do. The world isn't all bones and liver." And I hadn't been living with the man and Bill in their cottage long before I found out how right she was.

It was the man's shyness that made all the trouble. It seemed as if he hated to be taken notice of.

It started on my very first night at the cottage. I had fallen asleep in the kitchen, tired out after all the excitement of the day and the long walks I had had, when something woke me with a start. It was somebody scratching at the window, trying to get in.

Well, I ask you, I ask any dog, what would you have done in my place? Ever since I was old enough to listen, mother had told me over and over again what I must do in a case like this. It is the A B C of a dog's education. "If you are in a room and you hear anyone trying to get in," mother used to say, "bark. It may be someone who has business there, or it may not. Bark first, and inquire afterwards. Dogs were made to be heard and not seen."

I lifted my head and yelled. I have a good, deep voice, due to a hound strain in my pedigree, and at the public-house, when there was a full moon, I have often had people leaning out of the windows and saying things all down the street. I took a deep breath and let it go.

"Man!" I shouted. "Bill! Man! Come quick! Here's a burglar getting in!"

Then somebody struck a light, and it was the man himself. He had come in through the window.

He picked up a stick, and he walloped me. I couldn't understand it. I couldn't see where I had done the wrong thing. But he was the boss, so there was nothing to be said.

If you'll believe me, that same thing happened every night. Every single night! And sometimes twice or three times before morning. And every time I would bark my loudest, and the man would strike a light and wallop me. The thing was baffling. I couldn't possibly have mistaken what mother had said to me. She said it too often for that. Bark! Bark! Bark! It was the main plank of her whole system of education. And yet, here I was, getting walloped every night for doing it.

I thought it out till my head ached, and finally I got it right. I began to see that mother's outlook was narrow. No doubt, living with a man like master at the public-house, a man without a trace of shyness in his composition, barking was all right. But circumstances alter cases. I belonged to a man who was a mass of nerves, who got the jumps if you spoke to him. What I had to do was to forget the training I had had from mother, sound as it no doubt was as a general thing, and to adapt myself to the needs of the particular man who had happened to buy me. I had tried mother's way, and all it had brought me was walloping, so now I would think for myself.

So next night, when I heard the window go, I lay there without a word, though it went against all my better feelings. I didn't even growl. Someone came in and moved about in the dark, with a lantern, but, though I smelt that it was the man, I didn't ask him a single question. And presently the man lit a light and came over to me and gave me a pat, which was a thing he had never done before.

"Good dog!" he said. "Now you can have this."

And he let me lick out the saucepan in which the dinner had been cooked.

After that, we got on fine. Whenever I heard anyone at the window I just kept curled up and took no notice, and every time I got a bone or something good. It was easy, once you had got the hang of things.

It was about a week after that the man took me out one morning, and we walked a long way till we turned in at some big gates and went along a very smooth road till we came to a great house, standing all by itself in the middle of a whole lot of country. There was a big lawn in front of it, and all round there were fields and trees, and at the back a great wood.

The man rang a bell, and the door opened, and an old man came out.

"Well?" he said, not very cordially.

"I thought you might want to buy a good watchdog," said the man.

"Well, that's queer, your saying that," said the caretaker. "It's a coincidence. That's exactly what I do want to buy. I was just thinking of going along and trying to get one. My old dog picked up something this morning that he oughtn't to have, and he's dead, poor feller."

"Poor feller," said the man. "Found an old bone with phosphorus on it, I guess."

"What do you want for this one?"

"Five shillings."

"Is he a good watchdog?"

"He's a grand watchdog."

"He looks fierce enough."

"Ah!"

So the caretaker gave the man his five shillings, and the man went off and left me.

At first the newness of everything and the unaccustomed smells and getting to know the caretaker, who was a nice old man, prevented my missing the man, but as the day went on and I began to realise that he'd gone and would never come back, I got very depressed. I pattered all over the house, whining. It was a most interesting house, bigger than I thought a house could possibly be, but it couldn't cheer me up. You may think it strange that I should pine for the man, after all the wallopings he had given me, and it is odd, when you come to think of it. But dogs are dogs, and they are built like that. By the time it was evening I was thoroughly miserable. I found a shoe and an old clothes-brush in one of the rooms, but could eat nothing. I just sat and moped.

It's a funny thing, but it seems as if it always happens that just when you are feeling most miserable, something nice happens. As I sat there, there came from outside the sound of a motor-bicycle, and somebody shouted.

It was dear old Fred, my old pal Fred, the best old boy that ever stepped. I recognised his voice in a second, and I was scratching at the door before the old man had time to get up out of his chair.

Well, well, well! That was a pleasant surprise! I ran five times round the lawn without stopping, and then I came back and jumped up at him.

"What are you doing here, Fred?" I said. "Is this caretaker your father? Have you seen the rabbits in the wood? How long are you going to stop? How's mother? I like the country. Have you come all the way from the public-house? I'm living here now. Your father gave five shillings for me. That's twice as much as I was worth when I saw you last."

"Why, it's young Nigger!" That was what they called me at the saloon. "What are you doing here? Where did you get this dog, father?"

"A man sold him to me this morning. Poor old Bob got poisoned. This one ought to be just as good a watchdog. He barks loud enough."

"He should be. His mother is the best watchdog in London. This cheese-hound used to belong to the boss. Funny him getting down here."

We went into the house and had supper. And after supper we sat and talked. Fred was only down for the night, he said, because the boss wanted him back next day.

"And I'd sooner have my job, than yours, dad," he said. "Of all the lonely places! I wonder you aren't scared of burglars."

"I've my shot-gun, and there's the dog. I might be scared if it wasn't for him, but he kind of gives me confidence. Old Bob was the same. Dogs are a comfort in the country."

"Get many tramps here?"

"I've only seen one in two months, and that's the feller who sold me the dog here."

As they were talking about the man, I asked Fred if he knew him. They might have met at the public-house, when the man was buying me from the boss.

"You would like him," I said. "I wish you could have met."

"What's he growling at?" asked Fred. "Think he heard something?"

The old man laughed.

"He wasn't growling. He was talking in his sleep. You're nervous, Fred. It comes of living in the city."

"Well, I am. I like this place in the daytime, but it gives me the pip at night. It's so quiet. How you can stand it here all the time, I can't understand. Two nights of it would have me seeing things."

His father laughed.

"If you feel like that, Fred, you had better take the gun to bed with you. I shall be quite happy without it."

"I will," said Fred. "I'll take six if you've got them."

And after that they went upstairs. I had a basket in the hall, which had belonged to Bob, the dog who had got poisoned. It was a comfortable basket, but I was so excited at having met Fred again that I couldn't sleep.

Besides, there was a smell of mice somewhere, and I had to move around, trying to place it.

I was just sniffing at a place in the wall, when I heard a scratching noise. At first I thought it was the mice working in a different place, but, when I listened, I found that the sound came from the window. Somebody was doing something to it from the outside.

If it had been mother, she would have lifted the roof off right there, and so should I, if it hadn't been for what the man had taught me. I didn't think it possible that this could be the man come back, for he had gone away and said nothing about ever seeing me again. But I didn't bark. I stopped where I was and listened. And presently the window came open, and somebody began to climb in.

I gave a good sniff, and I knew it was the man.

I was so delighted that for a moment I nearly forgot myself and shouted with joy, but I remembered in time how shy he was, and stopped myself. But I ran to him and jumped up quite quietly, and he told me to lie down. I was disappointed that he didn't seem more pleased to see me. I lay down.

It was very dark, but he had brought a lantern with him, and I could see him moving about the room, picking things up and putting them in a bag which he had brought with him. Every now and then he would stop and listen, and then he would start moving round again. He was very quick about it, but very quiet. It was plain that he didn't want Fred or his father to come down and find him.

I kept thinking about this peculiarity of his while I watched him. I suppose, being chummy myself, I find it hard to understand that everybody else in the world isn't chummy too. Of course, my experience at the public-house had taught me that men are just as different from each other as dogs. If I chewed master's shoe, for instance, he used to kick me; but if I chewed Fred's, Fred would tickle me under the ear. And, similarly, some men are shy and some men are mixers. I quite appreciated that, but I couldn't help feeling that the man carried shyness to a point where it became morbid. And he didn't give himself a chance to cure himself of it. That was the point. Imagine a man hating to meet people so much that he never visited their houses till the middle of the night, when they were in bed and asleep. It was silly. Shyness has always been something so outside my nature that I suppose I have never really been able to look at it sympathetically. I have always held the view that you can get over it if you make an effort. The trouble with the man was that he wouldn't make an effort. He went out of his way to avoid meeting people.

I was fond of the man. He was the sort of person you never got to know very well, but we had been together for quite a while, and I wouldn't have been a dog if I hadn't got attached to him.

As I sat and watched him creep about the room, it suddenly came to me that here was a chance of doing him a real good turn in spite of himself. Fred was upstairs, and Fred, as I knew by experience, was the easiest man to get along with in the world. Nobody could be shy with Fred. I felt that if only I could bring him and the man together, they would get along splendidly, and it would teach the man not to be silly and avoid people. It would help to give him the confidence which he needed. I had seen him with Bill, and I knew that he could be perfectly natural and easy when he liked.

It was true that the man might object at first, but after a while he would see that I had acted simply for his good, and would be grateful.

The difficulty was, how to get Fred down without scaring the man. I knew that if I shouted he wouldn't wait, but would be out of the window and away before Fred could get there. What I had to do was to go to Fred's room, explain the whole situation quietly to him, and ask him to come down and make himself pleasant.

The man was far too busy to pay any attention to me. He was kneeling in a corner with his back to me, putting something in his bag. I seized the opportunity to steal softly from the room.

Fred's door was shut, and I could hear him snoring. I scratched gently, and then harder, till I heard the snores stop. He got out of bed and opened the door.

"Don't make a noise," I whispered. "Come on downstairs. I want you to meet a friend of mine."

At first he was quite peevish.

"What's the idea," he said, "coming and spoiling a man's beauty-sleep? Get out."

He actually started to go back into the room.

"No, honestly, Fred," I said, "I'm not fooling you. There

is a man downstairs. He got in through the window. I want you to meet him. He's very shy, and I think it will do him good to have a chat with you."

"What are you whining about?" Fred began, and then he broke off suddenly and listened. We could both hear the man's footsteps as he moved about.

Fred jumped back into the room. He came out carrying something. He didn't say any more, but started to go downstairs, very quiet, and I went after him.

There was the man, still putting things in his bag. I was just going to introduce Fred, when Fred, the silly ass, gave a great yell.

I could have bitten him.

"What did you want to do that for, you chump?" I said. "I told you he was shy. Now you've scared him."

He certainly had. The man was out of the window quicker than you would have believed possible. He just flew out. I called after him that it was only Fred and me, but at that moment a gun went off with a tremendous bang, so he couldn't have heard me.

I was pretty sick about it. The whole thing had gone wrong. Fred seemed to have lost his head entirely. He was behaving like a perfect ass. Naturally the man had been frightened with him carrying on in that way. I jumped out of the window to see if I could find the man and explain, but he was gone. Fred jumped out after me, and nearly squashed me.

It was pitch dark out there. I couldn't see a thing. But I knew the man could not have gone far, or I should have heard him. I started to sniff round on the chance of picking up his trail. It wasn't long before I struck it.

Fred's father had come down now, and they were running about. The old man had a light. I followed the trail, and it ended at a large cedar-tree, not far from the house. I stood underneath it and looked up, but of course I could not see anything.

"Are you up there?" I shouted. "There's nothing to be scared at. It was only Fred. He's an old pal of mine. He works at the place where you bought me. His gun went off by accident. He won't hurt you."

There wasn't a sound. I began to think I must have made a mistake.

"He's got away," I heard Fred say to his father and, just as he said it I caught a faint sound of someone moving in the branches above me.

"No he hasn't!" I shouted. "He's up this tree."

"I believe the dog's found him, dad!"

"Yes, he's up here. Come along and meet him."

Fred came to the foot of the tree.

"You up there," he said, "come along down."

Not a sound from the tree.

"It's all right," I explained, "he is up there, but he's very shy. Ask him again."

"All right," said Fred. "Stay there if you want to. But I'm going to shoot off this gun into the branches just for fun."

And then the man started to come down. As soon as he touched the ground I jumped up at him.

"This is fine!" I said. "Here's my friend Fred. You'll like him."

But it wasn't any good. They didn't get along together at all. They hardly spoke. The man went into the house, and Fred went after him, carrying his gun. And when they got into the house it was just the same. The man sat in one chair, and Fred sat in another, and after a long time some men came in a motor-car, and the man went away with them. He didn't say goodbye to me.

When he had gone, Fred and his father made a great fuss of me. I couldn't understand it. Men are so odd. The man wasn't a bit pleased that I had brought him and Fred together, but Fred seemed as if he couldn't do enough for me for having introduced him to the man. However, Fred's father produced some cold ham — my favourite dish — and gave me quite a lot of it, so I stopped worrying over the thing. As mother used to say, "Don't bother your head about what doesn't concern you. The only thing a dog need concern himself with is the bill-of-fare. Eat your bun, and don't make yourself busy about other people's affairs." Mother's was in some ways a narrow outlook, but she had a great fund of sterling common sense.

Lenny's Red-Letter Day

Bernard Ashley

Lenny Fraser is a boy in my class. Well, he's a boy in my class when he comes. But to tell the truth, he doesn't come very often. He stays away from school for a week at a time, and I'll tell you where he is. He's at the shops, stealing things sometimes, but mainly just opening the doors for people. He does it to keep himself warm. I've seen him in our shop. When he opens the door for someone, he stands around inside till he gets sent out. Of course, it's quite warm enough in school, but he hates coming. He's always got long, tangled hair, not very clean, and his clothes are too big or too small, and they call him 'Flea-bag'. He sits at a desk without a partner, and no one wants to hold his hand in games. All right, they're not to blame; but he isn't, either. His mother never gets up in the morning, and his house is dirty. It's a house that everybody runs past very quickly.

But Lenny makes me laugh a lot. In the playground he's always saying funny things out of the corner of his mouth. He doesn't smile when he does it. He says these funny things as if he's complaining. For example, when Mr. Cox the deputy head came to school in his new car, Lenny came too, that day; but he didn't join in all the admiration. He looked at the little car and said to me, "Anyone missing a skateboard?"

He misses all the really good things, though — the School Journeys and the outing. And it was a big shame about his birthday.

It happens like this with birthdays in our class. Miss Blake lets everyone bring their cards and perhaps a small present to show the others. Then everyone sings 'Happy Birthday' and we give them bumps in the playground. If people can't bring a present, they tell everyone what they've got instead. I happen to know some people make up the things that they've got just to be up with the others, but Miss Blake says it's good to share our Red-Letter Days.

I didn't know about these Red-Letter Days before. I thought they were something special in the post, like my dad handles in his Post Office in the shop. But Miss Blake told us they are red printed words in the prayer books, meaning special days.

Well, what I'm telling you is that Lenny came to school on his birthday this year. Of course, he didn't tell us it was his birthday, and, as it all worked out, it would have been better if Miss Blake hadn't noticed it in the register. But, "How nice!" she said. "Lenny's here on his birthday, and we can share it with him."

It wasn't very nice for Lenny. He didn't have any cards to show the class, and he couldn't think of a birthday present to tell us about. He couldn't even think of anything funny to say out of the corner of his mouth. He just had to stand there looking foolish until Miss Blake started the singing of 'Happy Birthday' — and then half the people didn't bother to sing it. I felt very sorry for him, I can tell you. But that wasn't the worst. The worst happened in the playground. I went to take his head end for bumps, and no one would come and take his feet. They all walked away. I had to finish up just patting him on the head with my hands, and before I knew what was coming out I was telling him, "You can come home to tea with me, for your birthday." And he said, yes, he would come.

My father works very hard in the Post Office, in a corner of our shop; and my mother stands at the door all day, where people pay for their groceries. When I get home from school, I carry cardboard boxes out to the yard and jump on them, or my big sister Nalini shows me which shelves to fill and I fill them with jam or chapatis — or birthday cards. On this day, though, I thought I'd use my key and go in through the side door and take Lenny straight upstairs — then hurry down again and tell my mum and dad that I'd got a friend in for an hour. I thought, I can get a birthday card and some cake and ice-cream from the shop, and Lenny can go home before they come upstairs. I wanted him to do that before my dad saw who it was, because he knows Lenny from his hanging around the shops.

Lenny said some funny things on the way home from school, but you know, I couldn't relax and enjoy them properly. I felt ashamed because I was wishing all the time that I hadn't asked him to come home with me. The bottoms of his trousers dragged along the ground, he had no buttons on his shirt so the sleeves flapped, and his hair must have made it hard for him to see where he was going.

I was in luck because the shop was very busy. My dad had a queue of people to pay out, and my mum had a crowd at the till. I left Lenny in the living-room and I went down to get what I wanted from the shop. I found him a birthday card with a badge in it. When I came back, he was sitting in a chair and the television was switched on. He's a good one at helping himself, I thought. We watched some cartoons and then we played 'Monopoly', which Lenny had seen on the shelf. We had some crisps and cakes and lemonade while we were playing; but I had only one eye on my 'Monopoly' moves — the other eye was on the clock all the time. I was getting very impatient for the game to finish, because it looked as if Lenny would still be there when they came up from the shop. I did some really bad moves so that I could lose quickly, but it's very difficult to hurry up 'Monopoly', as you may know.

In the end I did such stupid things — like buying too many houses and selling Park Lane and Mayfair — that he won the game. He must have noticed what I was doing, but he didn't say anything to me. Hurriedly, I gave him his birthday card. He pretended not to take very much notice of it, but he put it in his shirt, and kept feeling it to make sure it was still there. At least, that's what I thought he was making sure about, there inside his shirt.

It was just the right time to say goodbye, and I'm just thinking he can go without anyone seeing him, when my sister came in. She had run up from the shop for something or other, and she put her head inside the room. At some other time, I would have laughed out loud at her stupid face. When she saw Lenny, she looked as if she'd opened the door and seen something really unpleasant. I could gladly have given her a good kick. She shut the door a lot quicker than she opened it, and I felt really bad about it.

"Nice to meet you," Lenny joked, but his face said he wanted to go, too, and I wasn't going to be the one to stop him.

I let him out, and I heaved a big sigh. I felt good about being kind to him, the way you do when you've done a sponsored swim, and I'd done it without my mum and dad frowning at me about who I brought home. Only Nalini had seen him, and everyone knows she can make things seem worse than they are. I washed the glasses, and I can remember singing while I stood at the sink. I was feeling very pleased with myself.

My good feeling lasted about fifteen minutes; just long enough to be wearing off slightly. Then Nalini came in again and destroyed it altogether.

"Prakash, have you seen that envelope that was on the television top?" she asked. "I put it on here when I came in from school."

"No," I said. It was very soon to be getting worried, but things inside me were turning over like clothes in a washing-machine. I knew already where all this was going to end up. "What was in it?" My voice sounded to me as if it was coming from a great distance.

She was looking everywhere in the room, but she kept coming back to the television top as if the envelope would mysteriously appear there. She stood there now, staring at me. *"What was in it?* What was in it was only a Postal Order for five pounds! Money for my school trip!"

"What does it look like?" I asked, but I think we both knew that I was only stalling. We both knew where it had gone.

"It's a white piece of paper in a brown envelope. It says 'Postal Order' on it, in red."

My washing-machine inside nearly went into a fast spin when I heard that. It was certainly Lenny's Red-Letter Day! But how could he be so ungrateful, I thought, when I was the only one to be kind to him? I clenched my fist while I pretended to look around. I wanted to punch him hard on the nose.

Then Nalini said what was in both our minds. "It's that dirty kid who's got it. I'm going down to tell Dad. I don't know what makes you so stupid."

Right at that moment I didn't know what made me so

stupid, either, as to leave him up there on his own. I should have known. Didn't Miss Banks once say something about leopards never changing their spots?

When the shop closed, there was an awful business in the room. My dad was shouting-angry at me, and my mum couldn't think of anything good to say.

"You know where this boy lives," my dad said. "Tell me now, while I telephone the police. There's only one way of dealing with this sort of thing. If I go up there, I shall only get a mouthful of abuse. As if it isn't bad enough for you to see me losing things out of the shop, you have to bring untrustworthy people upstairs!"

My mum saw how unhappy I was, and she tried to make things better. "Can't you cancel the Postal Order?" she asked him.

"Of course not. Even if he hasn't had the time to cash it somewhere else by now, how long do you think the Post Office would let me be Sub-Postmaster if I did that sort of thing?"

I was feeling very bad for all of us, but the thought of the police calling at Lenny's house was making me feel worse.

"I'll get it back," I said. "I'll go to his house. It's only along the road from the school. And if I don't get it back, I can get the exact number of where he lives. *Then* you can telephone the police." I had never spoken to my dad like that before, but I was feeling all shaky inside, and all the world seemed a different place to me that evening. I didn't give anybody a chance to argue with me. I ran straight out of the room and down to the street.

My secret hopes of seeing Lenny before I got to his house didn't come to anything. All too quickly I was there, pushing back his broken gate and walking up the cracked path to his front door. There wasn't a door knocker. I flapped the letter-box, and I started to think my dad was right. The police would have been better doing this than me.

I had never seen his mother before, only heard about her from other kids who lived near. When she opened the door, I could see she was a small lady with a tight mouth and eyes that said, "Who are you?" and "Go away from here!" at the same time.

She opened the door only a little bit, ready to slam it on me. I had to be quick.

"Is Lenny in, please?" I asked her.

She said, "What's it to you?"

"He's a friend of mine," I told her. "Can I see him please?"

She made a face as if she had something nasty in her mouth. "LENNY!" she shouted. "COME HERE!"

Lenny came slinking down the passage, like one of those scared animals in a circus. He kept his eyes on her hands, once he'd seen who it was at the door. There weren't any funny remarks coming from him.

She jerked her head at me. "How many times have I told you not to bring kids to the house?" she shouted at him. She made it sound as if she was accusing him of a bad crime.

Lenny had nothing to say. She was hanging over him like a vulture about to fix its talons into a rabbit. It looked so out of place that it didn't seem real. Then it came to me that it could be play-acting — the two of them. He had given her the five pounds, and she was putting this on to get rid of me quickly.

But suddenly she slammed the door so hard in my face I could see how the glass in it came to be broken.

"Well, I don't want kids coming to my door!" she shouted at him on the other side. "Breaking the gate, breaking the windows, wearing out the path. How can I keep this place nice when I'm forever dragging to the door?"

She hit him then, I know she did. There was no play-acting about the bang as a foot hit the door, and Lenny yelling out loud as if a desk lid had come down on his head. But I didn't stop to hear any more. I'd heard enough to turn my stomach sick. Poor Lenny — I'd been worried about my mum and dad seeing him — and look what happened when his mother saw me! She had to be mad, that woman. And Lenny had to live with her! I didn't feel like crying, although my eyes had a hot rawness in them. More than anything, I just wanted to be back at home with my own family and the door shut tight.

Seeing my dad's car turn the corner was as if my dearest wish had been granted. He was going slowly, searching for me, with Nalini sitting up in front with big eyes. I waved, and ran to them. I got in the back and I drew in my breath to tell them to go straight home. It was worth fifty pounds not to have them knocking at Lenny's house, never mind five. But they were too busy trying to speak to me.

"Have you been to the house? Did you say anything?"

"Yes, I've been to the house, but — "

"Did you accuse him?"

"No. I didn't have a chance — "

They both sat back in their seats, as if the car would drive itself home.

"Well, we must be grateful for that."

"We found the Postal Order."

I could hardly believe what my ears were hearing. *They had found the Postal Order.* Lenny hadn't taken it, after all!

"It wasn't in its envelope," Nalini was saying. "He must have taken it out of that when he was tempted by it. But we can't accuse him of screwing up an envelope and hiding it in his pocket."

"No, no," I was saying, urging her to get on with things and tell me. "So where was it?"

"In with the 'Monopoly' money. He couldn't put it back on the television, so he must have kept it in his pile of 'Monopoly' money, and put it back in the box."

"Oh."

"Mum found it. In all the commotion after you went out she knocked the box off the chair, and when she picked the bits up, there was the Postal Order."

"It's certainly a good job you said nothing about it," my dad said. "And a good job I didn't telephone the police. We should have looked very small."

All I could think was how small I had just felt, standing at Lenny's slammed door and hearing what his mother had said to him. And what about him getting beaten for having a friend call at his house?

My dad tried to be cheerful. "Anyway, who won?" he asked.

"Lenny won the 'Monopoly', " I said.

In bed that night, I lay awake a long time, thinking about it all. Lenny had taken some hard punishment from his mother. Some Red-Letter Day it had turned out to be! He would bear some hard thoughts about Prakash Patel.

He didn't come to school for a long time after that. But when he did, my heart sank into my boots. He came straight across the playground, the same flappy sleeves and dragging trouser bottoms, the same long, tangled hair — and he came straight for me. What would he do? Hit me? Spit in my face?

As he got close, I saw what was on his shirt, pinned there like a medal. It was his birthday badge.

"It's a good game, that 'Monopoly', " he said out of the corner of his mouth. It was as if he was trying to tell me something.

"Yes," I said. "It's a good game all right."

I hadn't got the guts to tell him that I'd gone straight home that night and thrown it in the dustbin. Dealings with houses didn't appeal to me any more.